Henry Charles Carey

Financial Crises

their causes and effects

Henry Charles Carey

Financial Crises
their causes and effects

ISBN/EAN: 9783337382254

Printed in Europe, USA, Canada, Australia, Japan

Cover: Foto ©Andreas Hilbeck / pixelio.de

More available books at **www.hansebooks.com**

FINANCIAL CRISES:

THEIR

CAUSES AND EFFECTS.

BY

HENRY C. CAREY.

PHILADELPHIA:

HENRY CAREY BAIRD,

INDUSTRIAL PUBLISHER,

No. 406 WALNUT STREET.

1864.

FINANCIAL CRISES: THEIR CAUSES AND EFFECTS.

LETTER FIRST.

DEAR SIR.—In your recent and highly interesting volume, which I have just now read, there is a passage to which, on account of its great importance as regards the progress of man towards an ultimate state of perfect freedom or absolute slavery, I feel disposed to invite your attention. It is as follows: " I am pained to hear such bad news from the United States—such accounts of embarrassments and failures, of sudden poverty falling on the opulent, and thousands left destitute of employment, and perhaps of bread. This is one of the epidemic visitations against which, I fear, no human prudence can provide, so far, at least, as to prevent their recurrence at longer or shorter intervals, any more than it can prevent the scarlet fever or the cholera. A money market always in perfect health and soundness would imply infallible wisdom in those who conduct its operations. I hope to hear news of a better state of things before I write again."

Is this really so? Can it be, that the frequent recurrence of such calamities is beyond the reach of man's prevention? To admit that so it certainly was, would be, as it seems to me, to admit that Providence had so adjusted the laws under which we exist, as to produce those "epidemic visitations" of which you speak, and of which the direct effect, as all must see, is that of placing those who need to sell their labor at the mercy of those who have food and clothing with which to purchase it—increasing steadily the wealth, strength, and power of these latter, while making the former poorer and more enslaved. Look around you, in New York, at the present moment, and study the effects, in this respect, of the still-enduring crisis of 1857. Turn back to those of 1822 and 1842, and see how strong has been their tendency to compel the transfer of property from the hands of persons of moderate means to those of men who were already rich—reducing the former, with their wives and children, in thousands, if not even hundreds of thousands of cases, to the condition of mere laborers, while largely augmenting the number and the fortunes of "merchant princes" who have no need to live by labor. Look around you and study the growth in the number of your millionaires, side by side with a pauperism now exceeding in its proportions that of Britain, or even that of Ireland. Look next to the condition of the men who labor throughout the country, deprived as they have been, and yet are, of anything approaching to steadiness of demand for their services, in default of which they have been, for two years past, unable suitably to provide for their wives, their children, or themselves. Study then the condition of the rich money-lenders throughout the coun-

(3)

try, enabled, as they have been, to demand one, two, three, and even four and five per cent per month, from the miners, manufacturers, and little farmers of the Union, until these latter have been entirely eaten out of house and home. Having done all this, you can scarcely fail to arrive at the conclusion, that unsteadiness in the societary movement tends towards slavery — that steadiness therein, on the contrary, tends towards the emancipation of those who have labor to sell from the domination of those who require to buy it—and that, therefore, the question referred to in the passage I have quoted, is one of the highest interest to all of those who, like yourself, are placed in a position to guide their fellow-men in their search for prosperity, happiness, and freedom.

The larger the diversity in the demand for human powers, the more perfect becomes the division of employments, the larger is the production, the greater the power of accumulation, the more rapid the increase of competition for the *purchase* of the laborer's services, and the greater the tendency towards the establishment of human freedom. The greater that tendency, the more rapid becomes the societary action — its regularity increasing with every stage of progress. In proof of this, look to that world in miniature, your own printing-office, studying its movements, as compared with those of little country offices, in which a single person not unfrequently combines in himself all the employments that with you are divided among a hundred, from editor-in-chief to news-boy. The less the division of employments, the slower and more unsteady becomes the motion, the less is the power of production and accumulation, the greater is the competition for the *sale* of labor, and the greater is the tendency towards the enslavement of the laborer, be he black or white.

The nearer the consumer to the producer, the more instant and the more regular become the exchanges of service, whether in the shape of labor for money, or food for cloth. The more distant the producer and consumer, the slower and more irregular do exchanges become, and the greater is the tendency to have the laborer suffer in the absence of the power to obtain wages, and the producer of wool perish of cold in the absence of the power to obtain cloth. That this is so, is proved by an examination of the movements of the various nations of the world, at the present moment. Being so, it is clear, that if we would avoid those crises of which you have spoken—if we would have regularity of the societary movement—and if we would promote the growth of freedom—we must adopt the measures needed for bringing together the producers and consumers of food and wool, and thus augmenting their power to have commerce among themselves.

The essential characteristic of barbarism is found in instability and irregularity of the societary action — evidence of growing civilization being, on the contrary, found in a constantly augmenting growth of that regularity which tends to produce equality, and to promote the growth of freedom. Turn, if you please, to the *Wealth of Nations*, and mark the extraordinary variations in the prices of wheat in the days of the Plantagenets, from *six* shillings, in money of the present time, in 1243, to *forty-eight* in 1246, *seventy-two* in 1257, *three hundred and thirty-six* in 1270, and *twenty-eight* in 1286. That done, see how trivial have been the changes of France and England, from the close of the war in 1815, to the present time. Next, turn to Russia, and mark the fact, given to us by a recent British traveller, that, in those parts of the country that have no manufactures, the farmer is everywhere "the victim of circumstances" over which he has no control whatsoever—the prices of his products being dependent entirely upon the greater or smaller size of the crops of other lands, and he being ruined at the very moment when the return to his labor has been the most abundant. Look then to the changes throughout our own great West in the present year—wheat having fallen from $1.30 in May to 50 cts. in July—and you will see how nearly the state of things with us approximates to that of Russia. Compare all this with the movements of England, France, and Germany, and you will, most assuredly, be led to arrive at the conclusion, that the stability whose absence you deplore, is to be sought by means of measures looking to the close approximation of the producer and the consumer, and to the extension of domestic commerce.

Five years since, British journals nearly all united in predicting the advent of a great financial crisis, the seat of which would be found in France and Germany. More careful observation might have satisfied them that the tendency towards such crises was always in the direct ratio of the distance of consumers from producers, and that the real places in which to look for that which was then predicted, were those countries which most seemed bent on separating the producers and consumers of the world, Britain and America—the one seeking to drive all its people into the workshops, and the other laboring to compel them all to seek the fields, and both thus acting in direct defiance of the advice of Adam Smith. The crisis came, spending its force upon *those two countries*—France, Belgium, and Germany escaping almost entirely unharmed, and for the reason, that in all these latter the farm and the workshop were coming daily more near together, and commerce was becoming more rapid, free, and regular.

Russia and Sweden have, however, suffered much—the crisis having become, apparently, as permanent as it is among ourselves. Why should this be so? Why should they be paralyzed, while France and Germany escape uninjured? Because, while these latter have persisted in maintaining that protection which is needed for promoting the approximation of producers and consumers, the former have, within the last three years, departed essentially from the system under which they had been so rapidly advancing towards wealth and freedom—adopting the policy advocated by those writers who see in the cheapening of the labor and of the raw materials of other countries, the real British road to wealth and power.

Throughout Northern and Central Europe, there has been, in the last half century, a rapid increase in the steadiness of the societary movement, and in the freedom of man—that increase being the natural consequence of increased rapidity of motion resulting from a growing diversification in the demand for human services, and growing competition for the *purchase* of labor. In Ireland, India, Spanish America, and Turkey, the reverse of this is seen—producers and consumers becoming more widely separated, and exchanges becoming more fitful and irregular, with growing competition for the *sale* of labor. Why this difference? Because the policy of the former has been directed towards protecting the farmer in his efforts to draw the market nearer to him, and thus diminish the wasting tax of transportation, while the latter have been steadily becoming more and more subjected to the system which seeks to locate in the little island of Britain the single workship of the world.

How it has been among ourselves, is shown in the following brief statement of the facts of the last half century. From the date of the passage of the act of 1816, by which the axe was laid to the root of our then-rapidly-growing manufactures, our foreign trade steadily declined, until, in 1821, the value of our imports was less than half of what it had been six years before. Thenceforward, there was little change until the highly-protective act of 1828 came fairly into operation — the average amount of our importations, from 1822 to 1830, having been but 80 millions—and the variations having been between 96 millions in one year and 70 in another. Under that tariff, the domestic commerce grew with great rapidity — enabling our people promptly to sell their labor, and to become better customers to the people of other lands, as is shown by the following figures, representing the value of goods imported:

1830–31	$103,000,000
1831–32	101,000,000
1832–33	108,000,000
1833–34	126,000,000

Here, my dear sir, is a nearly regular growth — the last of these years being by far the highest, and exceeding, by more than 50 per cent, the average of the eight years from 1822 to 1830. In this period, not only did we contract no foreign debt, but we paid off the whole of that which previously had existed, the legacy of the war of independence; and it is with nations as with individuals, that "out of debt is out of danger."

The compromise tariff began now to exert its deleterious influence — stopping the building of mills and the opening of mines, and thus lessening the power to maintain domestic commerce. How it operated on that with foreign nations, is shown in the facts, that the imports of 1837 went up to $189,000,000, and those of 1838 down to $113,000,000 — those of 1839 up to $162,000,000, and those of 1840 down to $107,000,000; while those of 1842 were *less than they had been ten years before*. In this period, we ran in debt to foreigners to the extent of hundreds of millions, and closed with a bankruptcy so universal, as to have embraced individuals, banks, towns, cities, States, and the national treasury itself.

That instability is the essential characteristic of the system called free-trade, will be obvious to you on the most cursory examination of the facts presented by the several periods of that system through which we have thus far passed. From more than $100,000,000, in 1817, our imports fell, in 1821, to $62,000,000. In 1825, they rose to $96,000,000, and then, two years later, they were but $79,000,000. From 1829 to 1834, they grew almost regularly, but no sooner had protection been abandoned, than instability, with its attendant speculation, reappeared — the imports of 1836 having been greater, by 45 per cent, than those of 1834, and those of 1840 little more than half as great as those of 1836.

Once again, in 1842, protection was restored; and once again do we find a steady and regular growth in the power to maintain intercourse with the outer world, consequent upon the growth of domestic commerce, as is shown in the following figures:

1843–44	$108.000,000
1844–45	117,000,000
1845–46	121,000,000
1846–47	146,000,000

We have here a constant increase of *power* to go to foreign markets, accompanied by a constant decrease in the *necessity* for resorting to them — the domestic production of cotton and woollen goods having doubled in this brief period, while the domestic production of iron had more than trebled.

Twelve years having elapsed since the tariff of 1846 became fairly operative, we have now another opportunity for contrasting the operation of that policy under which Russia and Sweden are now suffering, with that of the one under which they had made such rapid progress — that one which is still maintained by Germany and by France. Doing this, we find the same instability which characterized the periods which preceded the passage of the protective tariff acts of 1824, 1828, and 1842, and on a larger scale — the imports having been $178,000,000 in 1850, $304,000,000 in 1854, $260,000,000 in 1855, $360,000,000 in 1857, $282,000,000 in 1858, and $338,000,000 in 1859 — and our foreign debt, with all its tendency towards producing those crises which you so much deplore, having been augmented probably *not less than three hundred millions of dollars*.

Ten years since, there was made the great discovery of the Californian gold deposits—a discovery whose effect, we were then assured, was to be that of greatly reducing the rate of interest paid by those who labored to those others who were already rich. Have such results been thus far realized? Are not, on the contrary, our workingmen — our miners and manufacturers, our laborers and our settlers of the West — now paying *thrice* the price for the use of money that was paid at the date of the passage of the tariff act of 1846? Are not these latter, at this moment, paying three, four, five, and even as high as six per cent per month? Are they not paying more *per month*, than is paid *per year* by the farmers of the protected countries of the European world? That they are so, is beyond a doubt. Why it is so is, that although we have received from California five hundred millions of gold, we have been compelled to export, in payment for foreign food in the form of iron and lead, cloths and silks, more than four hundred millions — leaving behind little more than has been required for consumption in the arts. Had we made our own iron and our own cloth, thus making a domestic market for the products of our farms, would not much of this gold have remained at home? Had it so remained, would not our little farmers find it easier to obtain the aid of capital at the rate of six per cent *per annum*, than they now do at three, four, or five per cent *per month?* Would not their power of self-government be far greater than it is now, under a system that, as we see, makes the poor poorer, while the very rich grow richer every day? Reflect, I pray you, upon these questions and these facts, and then answer to yourself if the crises of which you speak are not the necessary results of an erroneous policy of which, during so long a period, you have been the steady advocate.

The history of the Union for the past half century may now briefly thus be stated : We have had three periods of protection, closing in 1817, 1834, and 1847, each and all of them leaving the country in a state of the highest prosperity — competition for the *purchase* of labor then growing daily and rapidly, with constant tendency towards increase in the amount of commerce, in the steadiness of the societary action, and in the freedom of the men who needed to sell their labor.

We have had three periods of that system which looks to the destruction of domestic commerce, and is called *free trade*—that system which prevails in Ireland and India, Portugal and Turkey, and is advocated by British journalists — each and all of them having led to crises such as you have so well described, to wit, in 1822, 1842, and 1857. In each and every case, they have left the country in a state of paralysis, similar to that which now exists. In all of them, the exchanges have become more and more languid, the societary movement has become more and more irregular, and the men who have needed to sell their labor have become more and more mere instruments in the hands of those who had food and clothing with which to purchase it.

All experience, abroad and at home, tends, thus, to prove that men become more free as the domestic commerce becomes more regular, and less and less free as it becomes more and more fitful and disturbed. Such being the case, the questions as to the causes of crises, and as to how they may be avoided, assume a new importance — one greatly exceeding, as I imagine, that which you felt disposed to attach to them when writing the passage which has above been given. To my apprehension, they are questions of liberty and slavery, and therefore it is that I feel disposed to invite you, as a friend of human freedom, to their discussion through the columns of your own journal, the *Evening Post*—that discussion to be carried on in the spirit of men who seek for truth, and not for victory. If you can satisfy me that I am in error as to either facts or deductions, I will at once admit it; and you, I feel assured, will do the same. As an inducement to such discussion, I now offer to have all your articles reprinted in protectionist journals, to the extent of 300,000 copies — thereby giving you not less than a *million and a half of readers*, among the most intelligent people of the Union. In return, I ask of you only, that you will publish my replies in your single journal, with its circulation of, as I am told, fifteen or twenty thousand. That this is offering great odds, you must admit.

It may, however, be said, that the replies might be such as would occupy too large a portion of your paper; and to meet that difficulty, I now stipulate that they shall not exceed the length of the articles to which answers are to be given — thus leaving you entire master of the space to be given to the discussion. Hoping to hear that you assent to this proposition, I remain, very respectfully,

Your obedient servant,

HENRY C. CAREY.

W. C. BRYANT, ESQ.

PHILADELPHIA, *December* 27, 1859.

LETTER SECOND.

DEAR SIR.—Allow me now to ask you why it is, that great speculations, followed by crises and by almost total paralyses, such as you have so well described, *always* occur in free trade times, and *never* in periods when the policy of the country is being directed towards the creation of domestic markets, and towards the relief of our farmers from the terrific taxes of trade and transportation to which they are now subjected? That such are the facts, you can readily satisfy yourself by looking back to the great speculations of the four periods of 1817, 1836, 1839, and 1856, followed by the crises of 1822, 1837, 1842, and 1857 — and then comparing them with the remarkable steadiness of movement which characterized those of the protective tariffs of 1828 and 1842. Study our financial history as you may, you will find in its every page new evidence of the soundness of the views of Washington, Jefferson, and Hamilton, Adams, Madison, and Monroe, each and all of whom had full belief in the accuracy of the ideas so well enunciated by General Jackson, when he declared that we " had been too long subject to the policy of British merchants"—that it was " time we should become a little more *Americanized*"—and that, if we continued longer the policy of feeding " the paupers and laborers of England" in preference to our own, we should " all be rendered paupers ourselves."

Why is all this? Why must it be so? Why must, and that *inevitably*, speculation, to be followed by crises, paralyses, and daily-growing pauperism, be the invariable attendant upon the policy which looks to the separation of the producer of raw products from the consumer of the finished commodities into which rude materials are converted? To obtain an answer to all these questions, let us look again, for a moment, to the proceedings connected with the printing and publication of the *Evening Post*. Dealing directly with your paper-maker, you pay him cash, or give him notes, in exchange for which he readily obtains the money — no artificial credit having been created. Place yourself now, if you please, at a distance of several thousand miles from the manufacturer, and count the many hands through which your paper would have to pass — each and every change giving occasion to the creation of notes and bills, and to the charge of commissions and storage; and you will, as I think, be disposed to arrive with me at the conclusion, that the tendency towards the creation of artificial credits, and towards speculation, grows with the growth of the power of the middleman to tax the producers and consumers of the world.

Seeking further evidence of this, let me ask you to look at the circumstances which attend the sale of your products. Now, your customers being close at hand, you are paid in cash—your whole year's business not giving, as I suppose, occasion for the creation of a single note. Change your position, putting yourself in that of the Manchester manufacturers, at a distance of thousands of miles from your customers, compelled to deal with traders and transporters, and study the quantity of notes and bills, with their attendant charges, that would be created—the augmentation of price and diminution of consumption that would be the consequence—the power that would be accumulated in the hands of those who had money to invest, and desired to produce such crises as those which you have so well depicted—and you will, most assuredly, arrive at the conclusion that there is but one road towards steadiness and freedom, and that that road is to be found in the direction of measures having for their object the more close approximation of the producers and consumers of the products of the earth.

Studying next the great facts of our financial history, with a view to ascertain how far they are in accordance with the theory you may thus have formed, you will see that, in those prosperous years of the tariff of 1828, from 1830 to 1833, the quantity of bank notes in circulation was but 80 millions. No sooner, however, had we entered upon the free trade policy, providing for the gradual diminution and ultimate abolition of protection, than we find a rapid growth of speculation, consequent upon the growing power for the creation of artificial credits—the average circulation of the years from 1834 to 1837 having been no less than 149 millions, or nearly twice what it before had been. Under the protective tariff of 1842, the average was but 76 millions; but no sooner had protection been abandoned, than we find an increase so rapid as to have carried up the average from 1846 to 1849, to 113, and that of 1850 and 1851, to 143 millions. In that period speculation had largely grown, but prosperity had as much declined. When the circulation was small, domestic commerce was great — mines having been opened, furnaces and factories having been built, and labor having found its full reward. When, on the contrary, the circulation had become so great, mines were being closed and miners were being ruined — furnaces and factories were being sold by the sheriff, and our people were unemployed. In the one case, men were becoming more free, while in the other they were gradually losing the power to determine for themselves to whom they would sell their labor, or what should be its reward. In the one, there was a growing competition for the *purchase* of the laborer's services. In the other, there was increasing competition for their *sale*. Such having invariably been the case, can you, my dear sir, hesitate to believe, that the question to whose discussion I have invited you, *is not* one of the prices of cotton or woollen cloths, but *is*, really, that of man's progress towards that perfect freedom of action which we should all desire for ourselves and those around us, on the one hand, or his decline towards slavery, and its attendant barbarism, on the other? That, as it seems to me, you can scarcely do.

At no period in the history of the Union has competition for the *purchase* of labor, accompanied by growing tendency towards improvement in the condition of the laborer, been so universal or so great as in 1815, 1834, and 1847, the closing years of the several periods in which the policy of the country was directed towards the approximation of the producers and consumers of the country, by means of measures of protection. At none, has the competition for its *sale*, with corresponding decline in the laborer's condition, been so great as in the closing years of the free trade periods, to wit, from 1822 to 1824, and from 1840 to 1842.

Great as was the prosperity with which we closed the period which had commenced in this latter year, three short years of the tariff of 1846 sufficed for reproducing that competition for the *sale* of labor, relief from which had been the object of the men who made the tariff of 1842. From the decline with which we then were menaced, we were relieved by the discovery of the Californian mines, and by that alone. Since then, we have thence received more than five hundred millions of gold, and yet at no period has there existed a greater tendency to increase of competition for the *sale* of labor than at present — the two cities of New York and Philadelphia, alone, presenting to our view *hundreds of thousands of persons who are totally unable to exchange their services for the money with which to purchase food and clothing.* Is it not clear, from all these facts, that —

First, the nearer the place of consumption to the place of production, the smaller must be the power of transporters and other middlemen to tax consumers and producers, and the greater must be the power of the men who labor to profit by the things produced?

Second, that the more close the approximation of consumers and producers, the smaller must be the power of middlemen to create fictitious credits, to be used in furtherance of their speculations?

Third, that the greater the power of the men who labor, and the larger their reward, the greater must be the tendency towards that steadiness in the societary action, in the perfection of which you yourself would find the proof of "infallible wisdom in those who conduct its operations"?

Fourth, that all the experiences of continental Europe, and all our own, tend to prove that steadiness is most found in those countries, and at those periods, in which the policy pursued is that protective one advocated in France by the great Colbert, and among ourselves by Washington, Franklin, Hamilton, Adams, Jefferson, and their successors, down to Jackson; and least in all of those in which the policy pursued is that advocated by the British school, which sees in cheap labor and cheap raw materials the surest road to wealth and power for the British trader?

Renewing my proposition to cause your answers to these questions to be republished to the extent of not less than 300,000 copies, I remain, my dear sir, with great respect,

Your obedient servant,
HENRY C. CAREY.

W. C. BRYANT, ESQ.

PHILADELPHIA, *January* 3, 1860.

LETTER THIRD.

DEAR SIR. — In one of his *Mount Vernon Papers*, Mr. Everett informs his readers, that —

"The distress of the year 1857 was produced by an enemy more formidable than hostile armies; by a pestilence more deadly than fever or plague; by a visitation more destructive than the frosts of Spring or the blights of Summer. I believe that it was caused by a mountain load of DEBT. The whole country, individuals and communities, trading-houses, corporations, towns, cities, States, were laboring under a weight of debt, beneath which the ordinary business relations of the country were at length arrested, and the great instrument usually employed for carrying them on, CREDIT, broken down."

This is all very true — a crisis consisting in the existence of heavy debts requiring to be paid by individuals, banks, and governments, at a time when *all* desire to be paid, and *few or none* are able to make the payments. That admitted, however, we are not, so far as I can see, much nearer than we were before to such explanation of the *causes* of crises, as is required for enabling us to determine upon the mode of preventing the recurrence of evils so frightful as are those you have so well described. Why is it, that our people are so much more burthened with debt than are their competitors in Europe? Why is it, that it so frequently occurs among ourselves that all need to be paid, and so few are able to pay? Why is it, that crises *always* occur in free-trade times? Why is it, that they *never* occur in protective times? Why is it, that it so frequently occurs that those who are rich are enabled to demand from the poor settlers of the West, as much *per month*, in the form of interest, as is paid *per year*, by the farmers of England, France, and Germany? These are great questions, to which Mr. Everett has furnished no reply. Let us have them answered, and we shall have made at least one step toward the removal of the evils under which our people so greatly suffer.

Let us try, my dear sir, if you and I cannot do that which Mr. Everett has failed to do—ascertaining the cause of the existence of so much debt, the constant preliminary to that absence of confidence which impels all to seek payment, while depriving so nearly all of the power to pay.

The commodity that you and I, and all of us, have to sell, is labor — human effort, physical or mental. It is the only one that perishes at the moment of production, and that, if not then put to use, is lost forever. The man who *does* put it to use, need not go in debt for the food and clothing required by his family; but he who *does not*, must either contract debt, or his family must suffer from want of nourishment. Such being the case, the necessity for the creation of debt should diminish with every increase in that competition for the *purchase* of labor, which tends to produce an *instant* demand for the forces, physical or mental, of each and every man in the community — such competition resulting from the existence of a power on the part of each and every other man to offer something valuable in exchange for it. On the contrary, it should increase with every increase in the competition for the *sale* of labor, resulting from the absence of demand for the human forces that are produced. In the one case, men are tending towards freedom, whereas, in the other, they are tending in the direction of slavery—the existence of almost universal debt being to be regarded as evidence of growing power, on the part of those who are already rich, to control the movements of those who need to live by the sale of labor.

Where, now, is debt most universal and most oppressive? For an answer to this question, let me beg that you will look to India, where, since the annihilation of her manufactures, the little proprietor has almost disappeared, to be replaced by the wretched tenant, who borrows at fifty, sixty, or a hundred per cent, *per annum*, the little seed he can afford to use, and finds himself at last driven to rebellion by the continued exactions of the money-lenders and the government. Turn, next, to those parts of Russia where there are no manufactures, and find in the free-trade book of M. Tegoborski his statement of the fact, that where there is no diversification of pursuits the condition of the slave is preferable to that of the free laborer. Pass thence to Turkey—finding there an universality of debt that is nowhere else exceeded. Look, next, to Mexico, and find the poor laborer, overwhelmed with debt, passing into servitude. Pass on to Ireland, and study the circumstances which preceded the expulsion, or starvation, in ten short years, of a million and a half of free white people—that expulsion having been followed by the passage of an Act of Parliament for expelling, in their turn, the owners of the land from which those laborers had gone. Look where you may, you will see that it is in those communities of the world which are most limited to the labors of the field, that debt is most universal, and that the condition of the people is most akin to slavery—and for the reason that there it is, that there is least competition for the *purchase* of labor. There, consequently, there is the greatest waste of the great commodity which all of us must sell, if we would have the means of purchase.

Turn, now, if you please, to Central and Northern Europe, and there you will find a wholly different picture—competition for the purchase of labor being there steadily on the increase, with constant augmentation of the rapidity of commerce—constant increase in the power to economize the great commodity of which I have spoken—and, as a necessary consequence, constant diminution in the necessity for the contraction of debt. Why should such remarkable differences exist? Because, in all of these latter countries, the whole policy of the country tends towards emancipation from the British free-trade system, whereas India, Ireland, Turkey, and Mexico, are becoming from day to day more subject to it.

Looking homeward, we may now, my dear sir, inquire when it has been, that the complaint of debt has been most severe. Has it not been in those awful years which followed the free-trade speculations of 1816–17? Has it not been in that terrific period which followed the free-trade speculations of '37 to '40—that period in which a bankrupt law was forced from Congress, as the only means of enabling tens of thousands of industrious men to enter anew upon the business of life? Has it not been in the years of the present free-trade crisis, which present to view private failures of almost five hundred millions in amount?

When, on the other hand, has there been least complaint? Has it not been in those tranquil years which followed the passage of the protective tariffs of '28 and '42? That it has been so, is certain. Why should it so have been? Because in protective times every man has found a purchaser for his labor, and has been thereby relieved from all necessity for contracting debt; whereas, in free-trade times, a large portion of the labor power produced has remained unemployed, and its owners, *unable to sell their one commodity*, have been forced to choose between the contraction of debt on the one hand, or famine and death on the other.

Look next, my dear sir, to our public debt, and mark its extinction under the tariff of '28 — its revival under the compromise tariff — its reduction under that of '42 — and then study the present situation of a national treasury that, in time of perfect peace, is running in debt at the rate of little less than $20,000,000 a-year!

Turn then, if you please, to our debt to foreigners, which was *annihilated* under the tariff of '28—swelled to hundreds of millions under the tariff of '33 — and since so much enlarged, under the tariffs of '46 and '57, that the enormous sum of $30,000,000 is now required for the payment of its annual interest.

France, with a population little larger than our own, and one far less instructed, maintains an army of 600,000 men — carries on distant wars —builds magnificent roads—enlarges her marine and fortifies her ports — and does all these things with so much ease, that when the government has suddenly occasion for $100,000,000, the whole is supplied at home, and without an effort. Belgium and Germany follow in the same direction — not only making all their own roads, but contributing largely to the construction of those which are used for carrying out the rude products of our land, and bringing back the cloth, the paper, and the iron, that our own people, now unemployed, would gladly make at home. They are rapidly becoming the bankers of the world, for they live under systems even more protective than were those of our tariffs of '28 and '42. We, on the contrary, are rapidly becoming the great paupers of the world — creating seven, eight, and ten per cent bonds, and then selling them at enormous discounts, to pay for iron so poor in quality that our rails depreciate at the rate of five, six, and even ten per cent a-year.

Looking at all these facts, is it not clear, my dear sir —

That the necessity for the contraction of debt exists, throughout the world, in the ratio of the adoption of the free-trade system of which you are the earnest advocate?

That the greater the necessity for the contraction of debt, the greater is the liability to the recurrence of commercial crises such as you have so well described?

That the more frequent the crises, the greater is the tendency towards the subjection of the laborer to the will of his employer, and towards the creation of slavery even where it has at present no existence? And, therefore —

That it is the bounden duty of every real lover of freedom to labor for the re-establishment of the protective system among ourselves?

At foot* is given, as you see, your notice of refusal to enter upon the discussion to which you have been invited. For a reply thereto, permit me, my dear sir, to refer you to the following exposition of your own views in relation to free discussion, given by yourself, a few days since, in the *Evening Post:*

"THOSE POLITICAL LECTURES.—As our readers know, a project has been under consideration to give a course of political lectures in this city during the present winter, and in which our prominent politicians of all parties were to be invited to take a part. We now understand that the scheme has fallen through, mainly because no single Democrat could be found who was willing to ventilate his party opinions, and maintain them, in connection with a series of similar addresses by Republican, Radical, and American speakers. We are assured that of twenty Northern and Southern Democratic statesmen, who have been invited, not one has accepted the invitation. It is proper to say that the signatures to the letter inviting speakers represented a number of our very foremost citizens, of all shades of politics. If a letter, so respectably signed as to guarantee every courtesy to all who took part in the course, failed to secure at least *one* speaker to uphold Democratic principles, we may safely suggest that the old *soubriquet* of the "unterrified Democracy" is a misnomer. We regret the failure of the proposed course of lectures, but are glad to know that many Republicans were willing to participate. Why cannot we have a few Republican speakers in an independent course?"

Obviously, these Democrats fear discussion. For years, they have been advocating doctrines that will not bear examination before the people. What, however, shall we say to the free-trade advocates? Is there any one of *them* that would accept a proposition like to the one to which you have here referred? Would they even accept an offer that was so much better than this, that it would give them, of cool and reflecting readers, *five hundred times as many* as you could give to any Democrat, of mere auditors? Would Mr. Hallock, of the *Journal of Commerce,* accept the magnificent offer I have made to you, which, thus far, you have not accepted? Would it be accepted by Mr. Greene, of the Boston *Morning Post?* Will you accept it? If you will not, can you object to the course of the Democratic leaders to whom you have here referred? Scarcely so, as I think.

Hoping to hear that you have reconsidered the question, and have decided to accede to a proposition which will enable you to address to *a million and a half of readers,* all the arguments that can be adduced in support of free-trade doctrines, I remain, my dear sir,

Very truly and respectfully yours,
HENRY C. CAREY.

W. C. BRYANT, ESQ. •

PHILADELPHIA, *January* 17, 1860.

---

* "MR. CAREY'S CHALLENGE. —Mr. Henry C. Carey, of Philadelphia, known by various works on political economy, has challenged Mr. Bryant, one of the editors of this paper, to a discussion, in the newspapers, of the question of custom-house taxation. In behalf of Mr. Bryant, we would state that challenges of this kind he neither gives nor accepts. It would almost seem like affectation on his part to say that he has not read the letters — two in number, he is told — in which this defiance is given on the part of Mr. Carey, having, unfortunately, too little curiosity to see in what terms it is expressed; but as such is the fact, it is well perhaps to mention it. His duties as a journalist, and a commentator on the events of the day and the various interesting questions which they suggest, leave

him no time for a sparring-match with Mr. Carey, to which the public, after a little while, would pay no attention; and if he had ever so much time, and the public were ever so much interested in what he had to say, he has no ambition to distinguish himself as a public disputant. His business is to enforce what he considers important political truths, and refute what seem to him errors, just as the occasions arise, and to such extent as he imagines himself able to secure the attention of those who read this journal, and he will not turn aside from this course to tie himself down to a tedious dispute concerning the tariff question at any man's invitation.

"The question of the tariff is not the principal controversy of the day. It may seem so to Mr. Carey, who is suffering under a sort of monomania, but the public mind is occupied just now with matters of graver import. To them it is proper that a journalist should principally address himself, until they are disposed of. He may make occasional skirmishes in other fields of controversy, but here is the main battle. When the tariff question comes up again, it will be early enough to meet it; and even then, a journalist who understands his vocation would keep himself free to meet it in his own way.

"If Mr. Carey is anxious to call out some antagonist with whom to measure weapons in a formal combat, and can find nobody who has an equal desire with himself to shine in controversy, we can recommend to him a person with whom he can tilt to his heart's content. One Henry C. Carey, of Philadelphia, published, some twenty years since, a work in three volumes, entitled 'Principles of Political Economy,' in which he showed, from the experience of all the world, that the welfare of a country is dependent on its freedom of trade, and that, in proportion as its commerce is emancipated from the shackles of protection, and approaches absolute freedom, its people are active, thriving, and prosperous. We will put forward Henry C. Carey as the champion to do battle with Henry C. Carey. This gentleman, who is now so full of fight, will have ample work on his hands in demolishing the positions of his adversary, with which he has the great advantage of being already perfectly familiar. When that is done, which will take three or four years at the least, inasmuch as both the disputants are voluminous writers, we would suggest that he give immediate notice to his associates, the owners of the Pennsylvania iron-mills, who will doubtless lose no time in erecting a cast-iron statue in honor of the victor."

LETTER FOURTH.

DEAR SIR.—In the notice of your refusal to enter upon the discussion to which you have been invited, it is said that you "had not read the letters" that had been addressed to you. That such had been the case, is not at all improbable; but how far a great public teacher, as you undoubtedly are, can be held justified in closing his eyes when invited to a calm examination of the question whether his teachings tend in the direction of prosperity and freedom for the laborer, on the one hand, or toward pauperism and slavery on the other, seems to me to be far less certain. Placed myself in his situation, I should regard it as one of great responsibility — one in which erroneous action, resulting from failure to give to the subject the fullest and fairest examination, would be little short of the wilful and deliberate commission of crime. That you agree with me in this, I cannot, even for a moment, doubt.

That you had not read the notice served upon me, I regard as absolutely certain, and for the reason, that its tone and manner are entirely unworthy of you, and you would not, I am sure, permit anything to be said by others for you, that you would not say yourself. Further, you are there placed in the false position of doing what I know you would not do—shrinking from responsibility, by permitting yourself to be presented to the world as being only "one of the editors" of the *Post*, instead of *the* editor, as you are so well known to be. Mr. Greeley is *the* editor of his paper, and, as such, endorses the opinions, given editorially, of the many gentlemen by whom he is aided. So, too, is it with yourself; and the rule of looking to the endorser when the drawer cannot be found, applies in this case as fully as it can do in that of a promissory note. So far as I can recollect, the editor of the *Tribune* has never shrunk from any such responsibility — having repeatedly replied, over his own signature, to papers addressed to himself in reference to editorials that he had published. Quite sure I am, that were you now to cite him before the world, as I have cited you, demanding an examination of the principles upon which he had based his advocacy of protection, he would most gladly meet you — giving to all you had to say the benefit of his enormous circulation, and leaving his readers to decide for themselves, after calm perusal of your arguments. Like you, he might find it quite impossible to give to the question all the attention it might demand, but, in that case, he would, most assuredly, find some one to take his place— becoming responsible, as editor, as fully as if he alone had written. Like him, you are surrounded by persons who have treated this subject on hundreds, if not even thousands, of occasions—you making yourself responsible for all they have thus far said; and I am, therefore, at a loss to understand why you should now fail to profit by the admirable opportunity offered you, for establishing the truth of free-trade doctrines. Can it be, that their advocates *dare not* meet the question? If so, are they not now placing themselves in a situation precisely similar to that so recently described by you, in speaking of your Democratic opponents?

2

I am told, however, that this is not the principal question of the day. It may not be so with the people of your city, but you would greatly err, were you to suppose that such was the case with those of the States south and west of you, and north of Mason and Dixon's line. In this State and Jersey, it is *the one*, and almost *the only* question. In Ohio, a large majority of the Republican senators are stated to have announced their distinct intention to make it *the* question. In Illinois, the most influential of all the Republican journals of the State has entirely abandoned the free-trade doctrines—giving itself now to the advocacy of protection. Throughout the West, the question of the adoption of measures required for the creation of domestic markets, and for the emancipation of the country from the control of British manufacturers, is rapidly taking the place heretofore so exclusively occupied by the anti-slavery one. All of these people *may* be wrong, and, if so, they should be set right. That they may be so, I have offered you the use of the columns of protectionist journals, circulating, to the extent of hundreds of thousands of copies, among the very persons who are thus in error. That great offer it is that, thus far, you have not accepted.

The great question of the day, in your estimation, is that of slavery and freedom, and in this we are entirely agreed. How is it that men may be made more free? That *is* the question, and it must be answered before we can venture upon action, unless we are willing to incur the risk of promoting the growth of slavery, while really desiring to advance the cause of freedom. All experience shows, that men have become more free as they have been more and more enabled to work in combination with each other, and that the power of combination grows as employments become more diversified—slavery, on the other hand, growing in all those countries in which men are becoming more and more limited to the labors of the field. Such being the case, that policy which tends to produce diversification and combination should be the one which would lead to freedom. Which of the two is it, protection or free trade, which tends in that direction? For an answer to this question, we need but look to Northern and Central Europe — finding there the protective system in full vigor, and the people rapidly advancing in wealth, strength, freedom, and power. The opposite, or free-trade system, has been in active operation in India, Ireland, Turkey, and other countries, whose people are as rapidly declining towards poverty, slavery, and general demoralization.

How, my dear sir, has it been among ourselves? Turn to the years which followed the abandonment of the protective policy in 1816, and study the rapid growth of pauperism and wretchedness that was then observed. Pass on to those which followed the passage of the protective tariffs of 1824 and 1828, and remark the wonderful change towards wealth and freedom that was at once produced. Study next the growth of pauperism and destitution under the compromise tariff, closing with the almost entire paralysis of 1840–42. Pass onward, and examine the action of the tariff of 1842 — remarking the constant increase in the demand for labor—in the production and consumption of iron, and of cotton and woollen goods — and in the strength and power of a community which had so recently been obliged to apply, *and that in vain*, at all the banking houses of Europe, for the small amount of money that then was needed for carrying on the government. Look, next, to the repeated crises we have had under the tariffs of 1846 and 1857—each and all of them tending toward strengthening the rich, while weakening the poor, and promoting a growth of pauperism such as has never, I believe, been known, in any country of the civilized world, to be accomplished in so brief a period. Such having been the result, the questions now arise, —Whither are we tending? Is it not toward slavery for the white laborer? Those are the questions I have desired to have discussed, and whatever you, my dear sir, may think of it, they must be always in order.

These, however, as may be said, are mere facts—a sort of *political arithmetic*. Trade should be free, and any facts that may be produced in opposition to that theory, must be such as cannot be relied on.—That we should be always going in the direction of freedom of commerce, and freedom of man, I fully and freely admit; but what is the road which leads in that direction? Certainly, not the one on which we recently have travelled—all our present tendencies being toward pauperism and slavery, for the white man and the black. As certainly, it is the one on which we travelled in the years of the period of the tariffs of 1828 and 1842; and if you desire any evidence of this, you have but to look to the most distinguished free-trade writers of the present century—their teachings and mine being in full accordance with each other.

Seeking proof of this assertion, allow me, my dear sir, to request that you will turn to *Mr. J. B. Say*, and study the cases described by him as being those in which "protection, granted with a view to promote the profitable application of labor and capital, may become productive of universal benefit." Look next, if you please, to *Mons. Blanqui*, his successor, and find him assuring his readers that "experience had already taught, that a people ought never to deliver over to the chances of a foreign trade, the fate of its manufactures." Pass on to *Mons. Rossi*, and read his entire disclaimer of the idea of non-intervention by the government—holding, as he does, that "a prudent and enlightened administration requires the making, in view of probable future benefit, of advances that may not, possibly, be repaid in full." Turn thence to *Mr. J. S. Mill*, who tells his readers, that "the superiority of one country over another, in any branch of production, often arises only from having begun it sooner, and that a country which has skill and experience yet to acquire, may, in other respects, be better adapted to the production than others that were earlier in the field;" but, that "it cannot be expected that individuals should, at their own risk, or, rather, at their certain loss, introduce a new manufacture, and bear the burthen of carrying it on, until the producers have been educated up to the level of those with whom the processes have become traditional." Look next to *Mons. Chevalier*, and learn that not only "it is not an abuse of power on the part of the government," but that "it is only the accomplishment of a positive duty, so to act at each epoch in the progress of a nation, as to favor the taking possession of all the branches of industry whose acquisition is authorized by the nature of things." The government which fails to do this, "makes," as he thinks, "a great mistake."

You have here, my dear sir, the views of five of the most eminent European economists of the present century—all of them high authorities in the free-trade school, and yet all concurring in the views I have expressed to you. Facts and theories being thus in opposition to your doctrines, is it not time that you should undertake anew the examination of the question, with a view to satisfy yourself whether the teachings of the *Post* are really those of slavery or of freedom?

I am told that I was once a free-trader, and nothing can be more true. Careful study of the phenomena of the free-trade convulsion of 1840–42, and of the protectionist revival of 1842–47, having, however, satisfied me that that the facts and the theory could not agree, I was led to study anew the latter, and find the cause of error. That found, I felt no more difficulty in admitting that I had been wrong, than would be felt by yourself, after you should have tried, and vainly tried, to establish the fact, that the cause of freedom was to be promoted by a policy that separated the producer from the consumer — placing the spindle and the loom on one continent, and leaving the plough and the harrow on the other.

At the moment of inviting you to join with me in an inquiry as to the real road towards wealth and freedom for our people, harmony for our Union, and prosperity and power for our great Confederacy — that inquiry to be conducted in the spirit of men who sought for truth, and not for victory — I had still some lingering doubts of your acceptance; and yet, it appeared to me that you yourself should be quite as anxious for it as I, by any possibility, could be.—Desirous to remove all difficulty, the space to be given was left to your decision — the greatness of the subject seeming to me to give assurance that the inquiry would be allowed to assume proportions somewhat in accordance with those of the interests to be discussed. Pledged, as we should be, to the cause of truth, and to that alone, any previous involvements, on either side, would shrink into utter insignificance. Neither of us, as it seemed to me, need be so anxious to shine in the dispute as to hesitate at any risk that we, as individuals, might run—pledged as we were, by all our past history, to give to this one great question, the most frank and candid examination.

Regretting that you have not, thus far, been able to agree with me in the view that has been here presented, but hoping that you may yet do so, I remain, with great respect,

Yours, very truly,
HENRY C. CAREY.

W. C. BRYANT, ESQ.

PHILADELPHIA, *January* 24, 1859.

LETTER FIFTH.

DEAR SIR. — A fortnight since, you stated, on the authority of Dr. Wynne, that pauperism in the State of New York had assumed proportions relatively greater than those of England or of Scotland, and "largely in advance" of even the downtrodden and unhappy Ireland—your percentage being as high as 7.40, or more than double that of all the British Islands. When these facts were first presented to your sanitary society, they appeared to the managers "so startling as to lead them to doubt their accuracy, but," as you now have told your readers, "after the most careful scrutiny, they have not only adopted them, but given them currency as authority in their report." This "condition of facts" is one that, as you think, "calls for investigation by the proper authorities" — the alarming facts being presented for their consideration, that no less than forty-one per cent of the paupers are native born, and that the terrible disease of pauperism appears, "like the Canadian thistle, to have settled on our soil, and to have germinated with such vigor as," in your opinion, "to defy all half measures to eradicate it."

The pauper is necessarily a slave to those who feed and clothe him, and a slave, too, more abject, as a general rule, than are even the negroes of the South. White slavery thus grows steadily — furnishing good reason for the fears that you have here expressed. Equal cause for such alarm may be found, however, in the fact that the growth in the number and power of your millionaires keeps even pace therewith—growing inequality of condition here furnishing conclusive proof of decline in civilization and in freedom. How is it that such effects are being produced? Here is a great question, the solution of which may, as I think you will agree with me, be found in the following frightful facts, which have just now been given to the world, and which reveal a state of things well calculated to carry the alarm of which you speak, into the breast of every man who takes an interest in our future.

In your city there are 560 tenement houses, containing, by actual enumeration, 10,933 families, or about 65 persons each; 193 with 111 each; 71 others, with 140 each; and, finally, 29, that, as we are told, are the most profitable, and that have a total population of no less than 5449 souls, or 187 to each. What are the accommodations therein provided for the wretched occupants, is shown in the following picture:

"One of the largest and most recently built of the New York 'barracks' has apartments for 126 families. It was built especially for this use. It stands on a lot 50 by 250 feet, is entered at the sides from alleys eight feet wide, and, by reason of the vicinity of another barrack of equal height, the rooms are so darkened that on a cloudy day it is impossible to read or sew in them without artificial light. It has not one room which can in any way be thoroughly ventilated. The vaults and sewers which are to carry off the filth of the 126 families have grated openings in the alleys, and doorways in the cellars, through which the noisome and deadly miasmata penetrate and poison the dank air of the house and the courts. The water-closets for the whole vast establishment are a range of stalls without doors, and accessible not only from the building, but even from the street. Comfort is here out of the question; common decency has been rendered impossible; and the horrible brutalities of the passenger-ship are day after day repeated, —but on a larger scale. And yet, this is a fair specimen. And for such hideous and necessarily demoralizing habitations,—for two rooms, stench, indecency, and gloom, the poor family pays—and the rich builder receives—'*thirty-five per cent annually on the cost of the apartments!*'"

We have here the type of the system that is now more and more obtaining throughout the country. One financial convulsion follows another, each in its turn closing mills, mines, and furnaces, and thus destroying internal commerce. With every step in that direction, our people are more compelled to seek the cities, and thereby augmenting the power of the rich to demand enormous rents, usurious interest, and enormous prices for lots—their fortunes growing rapidly, while reducing thousands, and tens of thousands, to a state of pauperism and destitution.

Is it, however, among the occupants of tenement houses, alone, that we are to find the facts which indicate the decline to which I have referred — a decline which *must* be arrested, if we desire not to find the end of our great republic is anarchy and despotism? Look around you, and you will see that while our population is growing at the rate of a million a-year, there is a daily diminution in the demand for skilled labor to be applied to the conversion of raw materials into finished commodities — a daily diminution of that confidence in the future which is required for producing applications of capital to the development of our great natural resources — a daily increase in the necessity for looking to trade as the only means of obtaining a support — and a consequent increase in the *proportions* borne by mere middlemen to producers, causing increased demand for shops, and stores, and offices, in great cities, and enabling landlords to demand the enormous rents which now are paid. The poor tenant slaves and starves, and finds himself at length driven to bankruptcy because his profits, after his rent is paid, are not enough to enable him to feed and clothe his wife and children —he and they being then driven to seek refuge in a "tenement house," there to pay a rent that enables its rich owner to double his capital in almost every other year. The rich are thus made richer, while pauperism and crime advance with the gigantic strides you have described.

Is it, however, in your city alone that facts like these present themselves to view? That such is not the case, is shown in the following accurate sketch of the Philadelphia movement in the same direction, given, a few days since, by your neighbors of the *Tribune:*

"Poverty has reached higher places in society than the habitually destitute. Want of employment with many, and reduced wages with others, all growing out of the warfare of the government on the industry of the country, have made the present season one of peculiar hardship and suffering. Honest labor goes without its loaf, because no one can afford to employ it. Persons formerly able to support themselves decently, are now crowding for relief to our benevolent institutions. The visitors of the latter say there is more suffering now than ever before known. Clothing, food, and fuel are daily given in large amounts, and yet the cry of distress continues. The soup-houses have been compelled to reopen, and the charitable are taxed to the utmost. These suffering thousands are the victims of the scandalous misgovernment which has palsied the energies of so many branches of industry. They would gladly earn their bread, if permitted to do so."

All this is strictly true, and it would, as I think, be equally so if said of any other city of the Union — the whole presenting a picture of enforced idleness such as is not, at this moment, to be paralleled in any country claiming to rank as civilized.   Pass next, if you please, outward from our cities, and look to the towns and villages of your own and other States — marking the fact, that the power of local combination is steadily diminishing, and that a majority of them have either become stationary, or have retrograded. - Go almost where you may, you will find that the internal commerce of the country is gradually declining — that the services of mechanics are meeting less and less demand — that the dependence on great cities is increasing in the same proportion that those cities are themselves becoming more dependent upon Liverpool and Manchester—and that, as a necessary consequence, pauperism and crime are everywhere assuming proportions so gigantic as well to warrant you in the assertion that their growth is now so vigorous as to bid defiance to "all half measures of eradication."

How may they be eradicated?   This is a great question ; but to find the answer to it, we must first inquire to what it is that such a growth is due.   Doing this, we find that the facts of the present day are in strict accordance with those observed in the years which followed the terrible free-trade crises of 1818–20 and 1837–40, as well as with those observed in Ireland, India, and all other countries subject to the British free-trade system.   Looking next to the periods which followed the passage of the protective acts of 1828 and 1842, we find directly the reverse of this — pauperism then steadily declining, and the morals of the community improving as the societary movement became more regular.   Turning thence toward Northern and Central Europe — toward that portion of the Eastern world which steadily resists the exhaustive British system — we find phenomena corresponding precisely with those observed in our own protective periods—the demand for human service becoming more and more regular in France and Germany, and the reward of labor growing with a steadiness that has rarely, if ever, been exceeded.—Such being the facts, is it not clear, my dear sir, that it is to the readoption of the protective policy we must look for effectual "measures of eradication."   Believe me, nothing short of this will do.

The readers of the *Journal of Commerce* have lately been assured "that our institutions nurture the evils in question."   Were that really the case, the evil would be so radical in character, that nothing short of revolution could produce the change desired.   That, happily, it is not so, you will, I think, be well assured, when you shall have reflected that all our institutions find their foundation in local development, tending to the creation of thriving towns and villages in the neighborhood of our vast deposits of coal and lead, copper, zinc, and iron—there making a market for the products of agriculture, and giving occasion to the improvement of our great water powers, to be used in the conversion of food and wool into cloth, and food, coal, and ore, into knives and axes, steam-engines and railroad bars. — What now is the object for whose attainment our people seek protection?   Is it not this very localization in which alone our institutions find their base?   That such is the case is beyond all question, and therefore is it, that confidence in those institutions grows in every period of protection — pauperism and crime then declining in their proportions with each successive hour.

What, on the contrary, are the tendencies of the British free-trade system? Do not, under it, towns and villages decline, while great cities grow in size? Under it, does not internal commerce die away? Do not crises become more frequent and more severe? Does not paralysis take the place of that healthy action which is indicative of strong and vigorous life? Do not pauperism and immorality grow with the growth you have so well described? Does not confidence in the utility and permanence of our institutions diminish with each successive year? To all these questions, the answers must be in the affirmative—such phenomena having presented themselves at the close of every free-trade period, and the only difference between the present and the past being, that the current one has been so much longer, and that the disease has, therefore, become by far more virulent.

Looking at all these facts, is it not clear, my dear sir —

That the cause of disease is *not* to be found in the character of our institutions?

That, on the contrary, it *is* to be found in the pursuit of a policy that is at war with those institutions, and threatens their destruction?

That the remedy of which you are in search, is to be found in the readoption of the policy of protection, under which the country so much prospered in the periods closing with 1834 and 1847?

That in default of the adoption of this remedy, our institutions must decay and disappear?

That every real friend of freedom should aid in the effort to rescue his countrymen from the grasp of foreign traders in which they are now held?

That every movement in that direction must tend toward diminution in the quantity of wretchedness and crime? And, therefore,

That all who oppose such action — teaching British free-trade doctrines — are thereby making themselves responsible, before God and man, for the demoralization above described?

Repeating, once again, my offer to place your replies to these questions within the reach of a million and a half of protectionist readers, I remain, my dear sir,

Very respectfully, your obedient servant,

HENRY C. CAREY.

W. C. BRYANT, ESQ.

PHILADELPHIA, *January* 31, 1860.

LETTER SIXTH.

DEAR SIR.—Pauperism, slavery, and crime, as you have seen, follow everywhere in the train of the British free-trade system, of which you have been so long the earnest advocate. On the contrary, they diminish everywhere, and at all periods, when, in accordance with the advice of the most eminent European economists, that system is effectually resisted. We, ourselves, are now in the fourteenth year of a free-trade period — the result exhibiting itself, as you yourself so recently have shown, in a growth of all that has at length most seriously alarmed the very men to whose unceasing efforts that growth is due. That they should be so is not extraordinary, but their alarm would be much increased were they now to study carefully the condition of affairs at the end of the peaceful and quiet period of protection which closed with 1847, and then contrast with it the state at which we have arrived — following up the examination by asking themselves the question — Whither are we tending?—and seeking to find an answer to it. The picture that would then present itself to view, would so much shock them, that they would shrink back horrified at the idea of the fearful amount of responsibility they, thus far, had incurred.

That the facts are such as you have described them, cannot be denied. Do they, however, flow necessarily from submission to the British system, miscalled by its advocates the free-trade one—that one which seeks to limit all the nations of the world, outside of England, to the use of the plough and the harrow, and to a single market, that of England, for an outlet for their products? That they do so, you will, I am sure, be ready to admit, after having reflected that men become rich, free, strong, and moral, in the ratio of their power to associate and combine together, and that the object of the British system, for more than a century past, has been that of preventing combination, by frustrating every attempt at the production of that diversification of pursuits, without which the power of association can have little or no existence.

What was the system before the Revolution, and what were the measures recommended as being those most likely to promote the retention of the colonists in their then existing state of dependence, are fully shown in an English work on the then American Colonies, of much ability, published in London at the time when Franklin was urging upon his countrymen the diversification of their pursuits, as the only road towards real independence, and from which the following is an extract:

"The population, from being spread round a great extent of frontier, would increase without giving the least cause of jealousy to Britain; land would not only be plentiful, but plentiful where our people wanted it, whereas, at present, the population of our colonies, especially the central ones, is confined; they have spread over all the space between the sea and the mountains, the consequence of which is, that land is becoming scarce, that which is good having all been planted. The people, therefore, find themselves too numerous for the agriculture, which is the first step to becoming manufacturers, that step which Britain has so much reason to dread."

Why, my dear sir, should Britain have so much dreaded combination among her colonial subjects? Why should she so sedulously have sought to disperse them over the extensive tracts of land beyond the mountains? Because, the more they scattered the more dependent they could be kept, and the more readily they could be compelled to carry all their rude products to a distant market, there to sell them so cheaply, as we are told by another distinguished British writer, "that not one-fourth of the product redounded to their own profit," as a consequence of which plantation mortgages were most abundant, and the rate of interest charged upon them so very high, as generally to eat the mortgagor out of house and home. In a word, the system of that day, as described by those writers, was almost precisely that of the present hour. For its maintenance, dispersion of the population was regarded as indispensable, and that it might be attained, the course of action here described was recommended :

"Nothing can therefore be more politic than to provide a superabundance of colonies to take off all those people that find a want of land in our old settlements; and it may not be one or two tracts of country that will answer this purpose: provision should be made for the convenience of some, the inclination of others, and every measure taken to inform the people of the colonies that were growing too populous, that land was plentiful in other places, and granted on the easiest terms; and if such inducements were not found sufficient for thinning the country considerably, government should by all means be at the expense of transporting them. Notice should be given that sloops would be always ready at Fort Pitt, or as much higher on the Ohio as is navigable, for carrying all furniture without expense, to whatever settlement they chose, on the Ohio or Mississippi. Such measures, or similar ones, would carry off the surplus of population in the central and southern colonies, which have been and will every day be more and more the foundation of manufactures."

Having studied these recommendations in regard to the maintenance of colonial dependence, I will ask you next to look with me into the working of the British free-trade system, and satisfy yourself that its advocates have been mere instruments of our foreign masters — closing our mills, furnaces, and factories, retarding the development of our great mineral treasures, preventing the utilization of our vast water powers, and in this manner driving our people to the West, in strict accordance with the orders of those British traders against whom our predecessors made the Revolution.

In 1815, the receipts from sales of public lands amounted to $1,287,000 This gives a measure of the then existing tendency toward dispersion. Five years later, when the free-trade system had paralyzed the industry of the country, they had risen to $3,274,000 — the customs revenue of the same year yielding more than $20,000,000. The government had seemed to be rich, and for the reason that it was "burning the candle at both ends" — paralyzing domestic commerce, and driving into the wilderness the people to whose efforts it had been used to look for its support. Free-trade excitement having been followed by paralysis, we find the customs revenue to have fallen, in 1821, to $13,000,000 — the land revenue at the same time gradually declining until, in 1823, it stood at less than a single million. As a consequence, we see the treasury to have been so much embarrassed as to be under the necessity of contracting loans, in the period from 1819 to 1824, to the extent of no less than $16,000,000. As usual, here and everywhere, poverty, distress, and debt, to both the people and the government, had followed in the train of the teachings of the men who had desired a readoption of that dispersive policy recommended by British writers, as a means of prolonging colonial dependence.

Turn now, if you please, my dear sir, to the picture presented by the protective tariff of 1828, and mark the steadiness of customs receipts, and the gentle and quiet growth of the receipts from lands, as follows:

	Customs.	Land Sales.	Total.
1829	$22,681,000	$1,517,000	$24,198,000
1830	21,920,000	2,329,000	24,249,000
1831	24,204,000	3,210,000	27,414,000
1832	28,465,000	2,623,000	31,068,000
1833	29,032,000	3,967,000	32,999,000

In this period, every man could sell his labor, and could therefore purchase the products yielded to the labor of others. Every one being thus enabled to contribute his share to the support of the government, the revenue had become so large and steady that the national debt was then extinguished.

Pass on now, if you please, to the time when the approaching annihilation of protection had stopped the building of mills and the opening of mines, and had recommenced to compel our people to scatter themselves over the great West, and find the following figures:

	Customs.	Land.	Total.
1835	$19,391,000	$14,757,000	$34,148,000
1836	23,409,000	24,877,000	49,286,000

Once again, the government was "burning the candle at both ends"—annihilating the power of combination, and thus diminishing the productive forces of the country. As before, it fancied itself rich, and acted accordingly—the expenditure of this period almost trebling that of Mr. Adams's administration, then but a few years past. As a consequence, bankruptcy of the people and of the banks was followed by disappearance of the power to contribute to the support of government, the customs duties of 1841 having but little exceeded $14,000,000, and the land sales having fallen to $1,300,000 — giving a total of less than $16,000,000, not even one-third of that of 1836. Such having been the case, need we wonder that the poverty of the government should have exhibited itself in the form of irredeemable notes, and in vain efforts to effect a loan in any part of Europe. Having destroyed our domestic commerce, and thus greatly diminished the productive power of the country, our foreign free-trade friends now turned their backs upon us — denouncing our whole people as rogues and swindlers.

Once again, in 1842, we find the readoption of the policy of resistance to British domination, and once again we meet the tranquillity and peace of the period which found its close in 1834, as is shown in the following figures:

	Customs.	Land.	Total.
1843-4	$26,183,000	$2,059,000	$28,242,000
1844-5	27,508,000	2,077,000	29,585,000
1845-6	26,712,000	2,694,000	29,406,000
1846-7	23,747,000	2,498,000	26,245,000

Again, as always under protection, there was economy in the administration of the government. Again, the necessity for contracting loans had passed away. Again, too, the foreign debt of the free-trade period was being diminished; and why? Because, once again, that colonial policy which looked to the dispersion of our people had been rejected. Not content with the lesson that had thus been taught, the protective policy was again abandoned, and once again we find the colonial system re-established, the results exhibiting themselves in the following remarkable figures, indicating the extent to which the government has recently been repeating the experiment of " burning the candle at both ends":

	Customs.	Land Sales.	Total.
1853–4	$64,224,000	$8,470,000	$72,694,000
1854–5	53,025,000	11,497,000	64,522,000
1855–6	64,022,000	8,917,009	72,939,000

As before, in every free-trade period, the government was becoming daily richer, while the productive power was declining from day to day. Expenditures, of course, increased — having reached, for those three years, exclusive of interest upon a large public debt, an average of $56,000,000, or nearly five times more than they had been thirty years before.

Having thus laid the foundation for a crisis, need we wonder that that crisis came, leaving the government, but recently so rich, in a state of actual bankruptcy, and wholly unable to meet the demands upon it? Certainly not. It was precisely what has happened in every British free-trade country of the world, and in every free-trade period of our own. In each and every one, our people had been driven out from the older States, and the government had been enabled to take from them, in payment for public lands, the mass of their little capitals, leaving them to borrow at three, four, or five per cent, per month, of the wealthy capitalist, all that had been required to pay for their improvements — and finally leaving them in the hands of the sheriff, under whose hammer their property had sold so cheaply as almost to forbid the purchase of lands that were as yet public and unimproved. The receipts from that source are now estimated at $2,000,000, and thus have we returned to a point that is really lower—our numbers being considered—than that at which we arrived at the close of the British free-trade speculations of 1817–18 and 1836–39.

Looking at all these facts, my dear sir, is it not clear —

That the system which you advocate, and which has usurped the free-trade name, is but a return to that colonial one described in the passages above submitted for your perusal?

That it has for its object the destruction of the power of combination, and consequent diminution of the ability to produce commodities in which to trade?   .

That, as a necessary consequence, it tends to produce a growing dependence of both the people and the State upon foreign traders and foreign bankers?

That to its present long continuance is due the fact, that British journalists now speculate upon "the recovery of that influence which eighty years ago England was supposed to have lost"?

That the tendency toward recolonization is growing with every hour, and that with each successive one, we are more and more becoming mere tools in the hands of British traders?

That, therefore, it is the duty of every friend of freedom and independence to lend his aid to the re-establishment of that protective system under which the country so much advanced in prosperity and power, in the periods which closed in 1816, 1834, and 1847?

Repeating the proposition, already so often made, to have your answers to these questions placed before a million and a half of protectionist readers, I remain, my dear sir, with great respect,

Your obedient servant,

HENRY C. CAREY.

W. C. BRYANT, ESQ.

PHILADELPHIA, *February* 7, 1860.

LETTER SEVENTH.

DEAR SIR.—The essential object of the British system, as you have already seen, is the suppression, in every country of the world, outside of Britain, of that diversity of human employments, without which there can be made no single step toward freedom. The more that object can be achieved, the more must other nations be compelled to export their products, and in their rudest shape, to Britain—doing so in direct opposition to the advice of Adam Smith.—This is what is called British free trade, the base of which is found in that annihilation of domestic commerce, whose effects exhibit themselves in the poverty, wretchedness, and crime of India, Ireland, Turkey, and other countries subjected to the system, all of which are so well reproduced among ourselves in every British free trade period. Real freedom of commerce consists in going where you will—exporting finished commodities to every portion of the world. Seeking that freedom, the most eminent French economists, as you have already seen, have held that it was "only the accomplishment of a positive duty" for governments "so to act as to favor the taking possession of all the branches of industry whose acquisition is favored by the nature of things," and that when they failed to do so, they made "a great mistake."

In full accordance with the idea thus expressed, the French Government has adhered to the policy of protection with a steadiness without example—the great result exhibiting itself in an export of the products of agriculture, in a finished form, such as can nowhere else be found. Thus protecting domestic commerce, the government finds itself repaid in the power to obtain revenue from a foreign commerce that has quadrupled in the short space of thirty years—the $100,000,000 of 1830 having been replaced by the almost $400,000,000 of each of the last three years—the population meantime having remained almost stationary. As a consequence of this the reward of labor has much increased, the people have become more free, and the State has grown in influence with a rapidity unknown elsewhere.

That it is to industrial development we are to look for the creation of a real agriculture, can now be no longer doubted—the Emperor having, in his recent letter, told his finance minister, that "without a prosperous industry agriculture itself remains in its infancy;" that "it is necessary to liberate industry from all internal impediments," and thereby "improve our agriculture;" and that in so doing the government will be "creating a national wealth" and diffusing "comforts among the working-classes."

Nothing more accurate than this could have been said by the great Colbert himself—the man to whose labors France was first indebted for the relief of her domestic commerce from the pressure of internal restrictions and external warfare. Compare it, however, I pray you, with our policy, erroneously styled the free trade one, every portion of which seems to have had for its object the creation of impediments to domestic commerce, and the subjugation of our farmers to the tyranny of foreign traders. Look, if you please, to the almost endless series of laws having for their object the compulsory use of gold and silver, in a country which exports the precious metals to such extent as to have driven our people, throughout a large extent of country, to the payment of three, four, and five per cent per month, for the use of the small amount of money which, even at such rates, can be obtained. Turn next to the postage law proposed by your Southern free trade friends, at the last session, by means of which the charge for the transmission of letters was to be almost doubled. Study then the constant succession of free trade crises, by means of which our domestic commerce has been so often paralyzed. Pass on, and find the closing of furnaces and mills, followed by constant increase of difficulty in the sale of labor — constantly growing pauperism and crime — and as constant increase of that dependence upon foreign markets which has, in every other country, been attended by growth of slavery among men, whether black, brown, or white. Look where you may, you will find the system of which you have been the steady advocate, leading to the adoption of measures directly opposed to the teachings of Adam Smith and those of his most distinguished successors, here endorsed by Louis Napoleon.

Turn next to another passage of the imperial letter, and find in it that agriculture must have "its share in the benefits of the institutions of credit," and that the government must "devote annually a considerable sum to works of drainage, irrigation, and clearage." Having read this, study, if you please, the proceedings of your free trade friends, constantly engaged as they have been, in the effort to destroy the credit of banks, and to prevent the substitution of paper for gold — and thus so far destroying confidence, that tens of millions of specie are now hoarded in private vaults by men who dare not spend it, and fear to lend it at any interest whatsoever.—Turn, thence, to the condition of our treasury, and contrast it with that of France — the latter proposing to lend money to the people at low interest, while the former is constantly in the market as a borrower, and at higher rates of interest than are paid by any government that claims to rank as civilized.

Pass next to manufactures, and find the Emperor telling his minister that, "to encourage industrial production, he must liberate from every tax all raw material indispensable to industry," and that he must "allow it, exceptionally, and at a moderate rate, as has already been done for agriculture, the funds necessary to perfect its raw material"—meaning thereby, as I understand it, further grants of aid similar to those which have resulted in improving the breed of sheep, and in giving to French agriculture many products not native to the soil, and yet essential to the perfection of manufactures.—Having studied this, allow me next to request that you will examine the teachings of the author of the tariff of 1846—the tariff you have so steadily admired—and find him protesting against the imposition of "higher duties upon the manufactured fabric than upon the agricultural product out of which it is made." Examine, then, his tariff, and find in it a systematic effort at the discouragement of industrial production by the imposition of heavy duties on the raw material of manufactures — sometimes so great. even, as to exceed those paid by the finished commodities for the production of which they were needed to be used. That done, look next at the repeated efforts of private individuals to improve our breed of sheep, and at the ruin that has been the consequence — that ruin having resulted necessarily from changes of policy that have closed our factories and sent merinos to the slaughter-house. Look in what direction you may, you will find that, with the exception of the brief and brilliant period of the tariff of 1842, the men engaged in the development of our great mineral treasures, and those engaged in introducing, extending, and perfecting works of conversion, and thereby giving the farmer a market for his products, have been regarded as enemies, deserving only of the hatred of the government; as men for the accomplishment of whose ruin fraud and falsehood might justly be resorted to — the holiness of the end sanctifying the employment of any means that might be used.

Adopting these ideas, the Emperor assures his minister that he will find in them the road toward real freedom of trade — the great extension of commerce producing a necessity for " successive reductions of the duty on articles of great consumption, as also the substitution of protecting duties for the prohibitive system which limits our commercial relations."— Having read this, do me the favor to turn to the period of the protective tariff of 1828, and find there precisely the state of things here described — the great increase of revenue having then produced a necessity for abolishing the duties that had always thus far been paid by tea and coffee. Look, next, to the working of that dispersive system, which scatters our population over the continent, and destroys the power of combination — at one moment filling the treasury to repletion by means of custom-house receipts and sales of public lands, and then leaving it bankrupt, to seek, as was done in 1842, and is now being done, for loans abroad, to keep the wheels of government in motion until the tariff can be raised.

The policy of the French Government was accurately defined, some three or four years since, by the President of the Council, and there is nothing in the Emperor's letter that is not in strict accordance with the determination then expressed, as follows :

" The Government formally rejects the principle of free trade, as incompatible with the independence and security of a great nation, and as destructive of her noblest manufactures. No doubt, our customs-tariffs contain useless and antiquated prohibitions, and we think they must be removed. Protection, however, is necessary to our manufactures. This protection must not be blind, unchangeable, or excessive; but the principle of it must be firmly maintained."

We are told, however, that a treaty has been signed, in which there are great advances toward freedom of trade. If so, it does but prove the perfect accuracy of M. Chevalier, who is said to have been the French negociator, in regarding protection of the domestic commerce as the real and certain mode of reaching freedom of intercourse with foreign nations. " In every country," as he has told his readers, " there arises a necessity for acclimating among its people the principal branches of industry"— agriculture alone becoming insufficient. " Every community, considerable in numbers, and occupying an extensive territory," is therefore, as he thinks, " well inspired, when seeing to the establishment, among its members, of diversity in the modes of employment. From the moment that it approaches maturity, it should seek to prepare itself therefor, and when it fails to do so, it makes a great mistake." This "combination of varied effort," as he continues, "is not only promotive of general prosperity, but it is the condition of national progress." Elsewhere, he says, that "governments are, in effect, the personification of nations, and it is required that they should exercise their influence in the direction indicated by the general interest, properly studied and carefully appreciated." Therefore does he "regard as excellent, the desire of some of the most eminent men of the principal nations of Europe to establish around them the various branches of manufactures."

Such being the latest views of the present leading free-trade writer of France, we may, I think, feel quite assured that what he may now have done, is only what he has regarded as warranted by the advanced position occupied by French manufactures — that position having been attained by means of a steady pursuit of the protective policy. It is the point at which we have ourselves arrived in reference to every branch of manufacture that has found itself efficiently protected in the domestic market, whether by the particular circumstances of the case, or by aid of revenue laws. More steadily than to any other, was protection given to the production of coarse cottons, and hence it is, that we now export them. The newspaper is protected by locality, and that protection is absolute and complete; and hence it is, that we have now the cheapest journals in the world. The piano manufacture is protected by climate; and therefore it is, that it has attained a development exceeding that of any other country. Had iron been as well protected, our annual product would count by millions of tons, and we should be now exporting, in the forms of iron, and manufactures of iron, a quantity of food twice greater than that we send to Europe. All our experience shows, that the more perfect the security of the manufacturer in the domestic market, the greater is the tendency to that increase of competition needed for enabling us soon to commence the work of supplying the exterior world.

In your notice of the changes now proposed in the French commercial system, you speak in terms of high approval of Mons. Chevalier, as a "zealous adversary of commercial restrictions," but have you ever, my dear sir, taught the doctrines of the teacher of whom you now so much approve? Have you ever told your readers,—

That "every community is well-inspired when seeing to the establishment among its members, of diversity in the modes of employment"?

That "combination of varied effort is the condition of national progress"?

That "every nation, therefore, owes it to itself to seek the establishment of diversification in the pursuits of its people, as Germany and England have already done in regard to cottons and woollens, and as France has done in reference to so many, and so widely-different kinds of manufacturing industry"?

That "governments are in effect the personification of nations, and should exercise their influence in the direction of the general interest, properly studied and fully appreciated"? And, therefore

That "it is only the accomplishment of a positive duty so to act, at

3

each epoch in the progress of a nation, as to favor the taking possession of all the branches of industry whose acquisition is authorized by the nature of things"?

Unhappily, such have not been the teachings of the *Post.* Had they been such—had your journal sustained the policy advocated by Mons. Chevalier, as here established at the date of the fearful financial crisis of 1842, should we not, even at this time, have been far advanced toward that position in which we could feel that protection would cease to be required? Unfortunately, it has taught the reverse of this—the results exhibiting themselves in a constant succession of financial crises, and paralyses of the most fearful kind—in repeated bankruptcies of the treasury, of banks, railroad companies, and merchants—in an almost entire destruction of confidence—in the subjugation of the poor borrower to the rich money-lender, to an extent unparalleled in any civilized country of the world—and in a growth of pauperism, slavery, and crime, that must be arrested if we would not see a perfection of anarchy established as being the condition of our national existence.

Had you and others taught the doctrines of M. Chevalier, would such be now the state of things in a country so richly endowed by nature as our own?

Not having taught them, and such having been the results of your past teachings, is it not now your duty, as a man, as a lover of liberty, and as a Christian, to study anew the doctrines of the economist you have so much commended, and satisfy yourself that you have been steadily advocating the extension of slavery while desiring to be the advocate of freedom?

Hoping that you may conclude to furnish answers to these questions, and reiterating the assurance that they shall have the largest circulation among the advocates of protection, I remain, my dear sir,

Yours, very truly,
HENRY C. CAREY.

W. C. BRYANT, ESQ.

PHILADELPHIA, *February* 14, 1860.

LETTER EIGHTH.

DEAR SIR.—For the maintenance of colonial dependence, and for the perpetuation of power to compel the colonists to make their exchanges in a foreign market from which they were allowed to carry away but one-fourth of the real value of their products, it was, as you have already seen, held that they should be led to disperse themselves throughout the West—thereby almost annihilating that power of association which, as then was feared, might lead to such increase of wealth and strength as would forward the cause of independence. For the accomplishment of that great object, the aid of government was then invoked—its help being needed for providing lands and means of transportation. Since then, the British free trade system has been employed to do the work, its mode of action being that one so well described in a Parliamentary document now but a few years old, the following extract from which is here submitted for your perusal:

"The laboring classes generally, in the manufacturing districts of this country, and especially in the iron and coal districts, are very little aware of the extent to which they are often indebted for their being employed at all to the immense *losses* which their employers voluntarily incur in bad times, in order *to destroy foreign competition, and to gain and keep possession of foreign markets.* Authentic instances are well known of employers having in such times carried on their works at a loss amounting in the aggregate to three or four hundred thousand pounds in the course of three or four years. If the efforts of those who encourage the combinations to restrict the amount of labor and to produce strikes were to be successful for any length of time, the great accumulations of capital could no longer be made *which enable a few of the most wealthy capitalists to overwhelm all foreign competition in times of great depression,* and thus to clear the way for the *whole* trade to step in when prices revive, and to carry on a great business before *foreign* capital can again accumulate to such an extent as to be able to establish a competition in prices with any chance of success. *The large capitals of this country are the great instruments of warfare against the competing capital of foreign countries,* and are *the most essential* instruments now remaining by which our manufacturing supremacy can be maintained; the other elements—cheap labor, abundance of raw materials, means of communication, and skilled labor—being rapidly in process of being equalized."

The system here so admirably described, is very properly characterized as being a "warfare;" and it may now be proper to inquire· for what purposes, and against whom, it is waged. It is a war, as you see, my dear sir, for cheapening all the commodities we have to sell, labor and raw materials—being precisely the object sought to be accomplished by that "Mercantile System," whose error was so well exposed in the *Wealth of Nations.* It is a war for compelling the people of all other lands to confine themselves to agriculture — for preventing the diversification of employments in other countries — for retarding the development of intellect — for palsying every movement, elsewhere, looking to the utilization of the metallic treasures of the earth—for increasing the difficulty of obtaining iron—for diminishing the demand for labor—for doing all these things at home and abroad — and for, in this manner, subjecting all the farmers and planters of the world to the domination of the manufacturers of Britain.

How our government co-operates in this warfare upon its people, and in the promotion of the great work of recolonization, will readily, my dear sir, be understood by all who shall study the British prescription given in a former letter, and shall then compare it with the course of action here, under your advice, so steadily pursued — expending, as we have done, and now are seeking to do, enormous sums, and even carrying on distant wars, for the acquisition of further territory — making large grants of land for facilitating the construction of roads and the dispersion of our people—forcing millions of acres upon the market, and then rejoicing over the receipts, as if they furnished evidence of increasing strength, and not of growing weakness — wasting the proceeds in political jobs of the most disgraceful kind, and in this manner producing financial crises that close our mines, furnaces, and mills, and drive our people to seek a refuge in the wilderness, there to pay the speculator treble price for land — and thus enabling him to demand three, four, or five per cent *per month*, for the use of some small amount of capital to aid in clearing the land thus purchased, and in erecting the little dwelling.—The house built, and the farm commenced, next comes the sheriff, and by his aid the poor colonist is now driven to seek a new refuge in some yet more distant territory — in full accordance with the desires of those of our free trade friends abroad, who see in every attempt at combination a step toward manufactures — "that step which Britain has so much cause to dread."

That such are the facts presented by our records cannot be denied. Having studied them with the attention they demand, you will, my dear sir, be in a position to answer to yourself, even if not to me, the question — Does the history of the world, in any of its pages, exhibit evidence of the existence elsewhere of so powerful a combination for the promotion of that pauperism and crime, whose extraordinary growth you have so well described? So far as my knowledge of history extends, it warrants me in saying, that no such evidence can be presented.

The poor colonist, thus driven out, suffers under a tax for transportation that, if continued, must for ever keep him poor. His need for better roads is great, but of power to assist himself he has none whatever. His distant masters may, perhaps, be induced to grant him help — knowing, as they do, that each new road will act as a feeder of their coffers, while aiding in the destruction of the powers of the soil, in the further scattering of their subjects, and in more firmly establishing their own security against the adoption of any measures tending to the promotion of industrial independence. Lands are now mortgaged, and at enormous rates of interest, as the only mode of obtaining the means with which to commence the road. The work half made, it becomes next needful to raise the means with which to finish it, and bonds are now created, bearing six, eight, or ten per cent interest, to be given at enormous discounts, in exchange for iron so poor in quality that it would find a market nowhere else — its wear and tear being such as must prove destructive to its unhappy purchaser. Under such circumstances the road fails to pay, and it passes into the hands of mortgagees, leaving those by whom the work was started, poorer than before — their lands being heavily mortgaged, and they themselves being at last driven out of house and home. Such is the history of most of the persons who have contributed toward the commencements of the road and canal improvements of which we so much boast, and such the history of the roads themselves — each and every financial crisis causing further absorption of American railroad property by English bondholders, as has been already done in reference to the Reading, Erie, and so many other roads.

Must this continue to be so? It must, and for the reason, that our whole policy tends toward the annihilation of local action and domestic commerce—that commerce in the absence of which railroads can never be made to pay interest on the debts to the contraction of which their owners have been driven. The greater their dependence upon distant trade, the more imperative becomes, from day to day, the necessity for fighting for it — for adopting measures tending to the further destruction of local traffic — and for thus rendering more and more certain the ultimate ruin of nearly every railroad company of the Union. How is it with yourselves — with the people of your State? But a short time since, we were assured that a barrel of flour could be transported to your city from Rochester at less cost than from Utica — from Buffalo more cheaply than from Rochester — from Cleveland for less than from Buffalo — and from Chicago more cheaply than from Cleveland — your railroad companies thus offering large bounties on the abandonment of the soil of the State, and thereby aiding our foreign masters in the accomplishment of the dispersion of our people. So is it in this State of Pennsylvania — through freight being carried at less than cost, while domestic commerce is taxed for the payment of losses, interest, salaries, and dividends.—In all this there is a tyranny of trade that has at length become so entirely insupportable, that the farmers of the older States are now clamorous for measures of relief — urging upon their respective legislatures the adoption of laws in virtue of which they shall be relieved from a tax of transportation that is destroying the value of their land and labor, and that must result in the crippling of all the Atlantic States, as well as of some of the older of their Western neighbors.

To such demand on the part of your farmers, you, however, reply, that it would be " legislation against trade" — that " nothing could be more impolitic than this process" — that

"The citizens of Baltimore and Philadelphia, if they should think it decorous and politic to do such a thing, might well pass a public vote of thanks to the legislature which would enact such a law. The moment it is passed, all the through trade, all the vast accumulations of the produce of the West which now find their way to New York by the New York Central Railroad, will desert it. When the Governor of New York signs the bill preventing free competition between our Central Railroad and its more southern rivals, he signs a bill for the relief of Philadelphia and the aggrandizement of Baltimore, and there will be great rejoicing in those cities, whether it be publicly expressed or not. . . . . . . The people of Maryland and Pennsylvania make no laws to prevent the competition of their railways with ours. They are satisfied to let those who manage them draw off as great a proportion of the freight from our channels of transportation as they are able, and they will be very glad of our co-operation in this work.

Baltimore has invested sixty millions of dollars in the railways which centre in that flourishing city. Whether these are profitably managed or not, is not so much the question with those who contribute the money, as whether the effect shall be to build up Baltimore as a great mart, and make Maryland the thorough-fare of an active trade. Baltimore is the commercial gate of the South; her ambition is to become that of the West also. No measure could be better calcu-lated to conspire with this ambition, and further this intent, than the *pro rata* freight bill now before our legislature. We earnestly hope that those members who have been induced to favor it will give the subject a more careful considera-tion, and spare us from an enactment the error of which will be but too deplorably evident before another legislature can assemble."

In all this, I find no single word in favor of the farmers and land-holders of your State — those people upon whom you so long have urged consideration of the advantage that must result to them from destroying internal commerce and readopting the colonial system against which our predecessors made the Revolution. Had you now occasion to talk to *them*, you would probably say — "Gentlemen farmers, you are entirely in error in supposing that you have any interests that require to be considered. The more you can be forced to become dependent upon Britain, the more rapid will be the growth of cities like our own. That the dependence may be increased it is needed that we close the mills, mines, and furnaces of the Union; that we render the laborer more and more dependent upon the capitalist; that financial crises con-tinue to increase in number and intensity; that the rate of interest be maintained so high as to ruin farmers, manufacturers, and railroad com-panies, while increasing the number of millionaires; that pauperism and crime continue to increase, with constant diminution in the power to purchase the products of the farm; that the productiveness of your land continue to diminish as it now is doing; that our people be dispersed; and that railroads continue to co-operate with the government in the effort to destroy that power of association to which, alone, should we look, did we desire to witness your growth in strength, wealth, and power. The heavier your taxation, the higher will be the prices of our city lots."

That the British free trade system is one of universal discord is proved by the commerce of India, Ireland, Turkey, and all other countries subject to it, and by our own, in every period of its existence. That opposition to it is productive of harmony, force, and strength, is shown in the movements of Germany, France, and every other country that looks to the development of internal commerce as furnishing the real base of an extended intercourse with other nations. Turn, if you please, to the recent letter of the French Emperor, and find him telling his finance minister that —

"One of the greatest services to be rendered to the country is to facilitate the transport of articles of first necessity to agriculture and industry. With this object, the Minister of Public Works will cause to be executed as promptly as possible the means of communication, canals, roads, and railways, whose main object will be to convey coal and manure to the districts where the wants of pro-duction require them, and will endeavor to reduce the tariffs by establishing an equitable competition between the canals and railways."

Compare with this the teachings of the *Post*, and you will find the latter saying directly the reverse—exhibiting the advantage of sending to England all our products in their rudest forms, thus losing the manure, and driving our people to the West, there to find a constant increase in the necessity for roads, accompanied by as constant decrease in the power to make them.—That done, allow me to ask your attention to the steady growth of harmony in the interests of railroad owners, farmers, and manufacturers, exhibited in the following figures representing the receipts of French railroads in recent years:

	Total Receipts. Francs.	Receipts per Kilometer. Francs.
1857	311,608,012	45,259
1858	335,289,015	41,398

The year following the great financial crisis exhibits, thus, a larger receipt than that by which it had been preceded. — Look now to the receipts of the first half of the two past years, as follows, and mark the great increase that has since been made —

	Total Receipts. Francs.	Receipts per Kilometer. Francs.
1858	148,955,578	19,805
1859	181,095,064	20,699

Compare, I pray you, my dear sir, the movement thus indicated with that exhibited among ourselves in .the past three years, and you will have little difficulty in comprehending why it is, that our railroad companies, like our farmers and manufacturers, our miners and our shipowners, are now being ruined — the $1200,000,000 expended in their construction having at this moment a market value that can scarcely exceed, even if it equal, $400,000,000.

Looking at all these facts, is it not certain, my dear sir, —

That the free trade system of which you are the advocate is one of universal discord?

That it tends to the involvement of men of all pursuits in life, and of the Union itself, in one great and universal ruin? And, therefore,

That it is to the interest of the railroad proprietor to unite with the farmer in promoting the adoption of measures having for their object the development of our mineral wealth, the creation of a real agriculture, and the extension of domestic commerce?

Hoping for replies to these questions, and ready to give them circulation among millions of protectionist readers, I remain, with much respect,   Yours, very truly,

                                                    HENRY C. CAREY.

W. C. BRYANT, ESQ.

PHILADELPHIA, *February* 20, 1860.

LETTER NINTH.

From the Evening Post, Tuesday, February 21st.

"AN ATTEMPT TO REVIVE AN OLD ABUSE. — It is intimated, we know not on what authority, that the Committee of Ways and Means are about to report a bill to the House of Representatives, with the view of carrying into effect Mr. Buchanan's recommendation to return to the old system of specific duties.

"If this be so, our aged President, who has been worrying about specific duties ever since he took the Executive chair, will undoubtedly enjoy a slight sense of relief. For our part, we should be perfectly willing to see him gratified in this respect, if the measure suggested did not imply an impeachment of the good sense of the committee by whom the bill is said to be preparing, and if the return to specific duties were not simply a device to increase the burdens of the people. The mill-owners are not satisfied with their profits; they do not make money enough by selling their merchandize, and they call for specific duties to enable them to extract a more liberal revenue from those with whom they deal.

"This is the plain English of the clamor for specific duties. The consumers do not want them, do not ask for them, are satisfied with the present method of collecting the duties by a percentage on the value of the goods imported; the only change they wish for is that the duties should be made lighter. Only the fraternity of mill-owners, shareholders in manufacturing corporations, capitalists who are anxious, as all capitalists naturally are, to make what they possess more productive than it now is, ask for the imposition of specific duties. They have not the face to ask for a direct increase of the duties as they now stand; they are afraid to demand that a tax of fifteen per cent on imported merchandize shall be raised to twenty per cent, or a duty of twenty to one of twenty-five or thirty. The country would cry shame on any such change. They, therefore, get at the same thing indirectly; they wrap up the increase of taxation in the disguise of specific duties; the consumer is made to pay more, but being made to pay it under the name of specific duties, the increase is of such a nature that it will be apparent only to an expert mercantile calculator. The consumer finds that the commodity he needs bears a higher price, but he is mystified by the system of specific duties, and does not know that the increase of price is a tribute which he is forced to pay to the mill-owners.

"That class of men who own our manufacturing establishments have had possession of the legislative power of the country long enough. It is quite time that the committees of Congress, and those who vote on the schemes laid before them by those committees, should begin to consult the wishes of the people. It is high time that they should begin to ask, not what will satisfy the owners of forges, and foundries, and coal-mines, and cotton-mills, and woollen-mills, but what is just and fair to those who use the iron, and warm their habitations with the coal, and wear the woollens and the cottons. This is not done; the lords of the mills speak through the mouth of the President of the Republic and call for specific duties, and now we are told that they are dictating a bill to the Committee of Ways and Means.

"Great apprehensions have been entertained by many persons, both here and abroad, lest minorities should be oppressed in our country by unjust laws passed in obedience to the demand of the mass of the people. We received, not long since, a letter from England, in which great anxiety was expressed lest this should lead to the downfall of our government. Hitherto, however, the people in this country have been oppressed by powerful and compact minorities. Laying aside the fact that small classes of men, united by a very perfect mutual understanding, and wielding large capitals, too often domineer in our State legislatures, it is certain that the revenue laws of this country have, for many years past, been framed by a minority. The mill-owners have dictated the whole system of indirect taxation, ever since the last war with Great Britain, and the utmost we have been able to obtain in the struggle against their supremacy has been some mitigation, some relaxation of the protective system — never a complete release from it. The oligarchy of slaveholders, scarcely more numerous than that of the mill-owners, and equally bound together by a common interest and concerted plans of action, have held the principal public offices, interpreted the laws, and swayed the domestic policy of the country with a more and more rigorous control for many years past. We are engaged in a struggle with that oligarchy now; but we have no idea of allowing the other oligarchy of mill-owners, while we are thus engaged, to step in and raise the tribute-money we pay them to the old rates. What we have wrested from their tenacious grasp we shall keep, if possible.

"Other governments are breaking the fetters which have restrained their peaceful intercourse with each other, and adopting a more enlightened system — a system which is the best and surest pledge of enduring amity and peace between nations. England and France are engaged in putting an end to the illiberal and mutually mischievous prohibitive system in their commerce with each other. It will dishonor us in the eyes of the civilized world if we, who boast of the freedom of our institutions and the wisdom of our legislation, should in the meantime be seen picking up the broken fetters of that system, and putting them into the hands of artisans at Washington to forge them again into handcuffs for our wrists. If any such bill as is threatened should be introduced into Congress by the Committee of Ways and Means, we trust that the Republicans of the Western States will be ready to assist in giving it its death-blow. If it do not meet its quietus from them, it will probably be rejected, as it will richly deserve, in the Senate, and Mr. Buchanan will never have the satisfaction of giving it his signature."

DEAR SIR :—You have been invited to lay before your readers the arguments in favor of such a change in our commercial policy as should tend to produce diversification in the demand for human service, thereby increasing the power of association and the productiveness of labor, while relieving our farmers from a tax of transportation ten times more oppressive than all the taxes required for the support of European fleets and armies — that invitation having been given in the hope that by its acceptance you would make manifest your willingness to permit your readers to see both sides — your entire confidence in the accuracy of the economical doctrines of which you have been so long the earnest advocate — and your disposition to espouse the cause of truth, on whatsoever side she might be found. That you should have failed to do this has been to me a cause of much regret, having hoped better things of a lover of freedom like yourself. Resolved, however, that *my* readers shall have full opportunity to judge for themselves, I now, as you see, place within the reach of the great mass of the protectionists of the Union, the reply that you have just now published, sincerely hoping that they may give to it the most careful study, and thus enable themselves to form a correct estimate of the sort of arguments usually adduced in support of that British free trade policy which has for its object the limitation of our farmers to a single and distant market for their products — the maintenance of the existing terrific tax of transportation — and the ultimate reduction of our whole people to that state of colonial dependence from which we were rescued by the men who made the revolution.

As presented by me, the question we are discussing is not of the prices of cotton goods, but of human freedom, and in that light it is that I have begged you should consider it. In support of that view, I have urged upon your consideration the facts, that every British free trade period has closed with one of those fearful crises whose sad effects you have so well depicted; that crises have been followed by paralyses of the domestic commerce, destroying the demand for labor; and that, as a necessary consequence, each such period has been marked, on one side, by a great increase in the number of millionaires, and on the other, by such a growth of pauperism that that terrible disease appears now, to use your own words, "like the Canadian thistle, to have settled on our soil, and to have germinated with such vigor, as to defy all half measures to eradicate it." Further, you have been asked to look to the facts, that the reverse of all this has been experienced in every period of the protective system — domestic commerce having then grown rapidly, with constant increase in the demand for labor, and as constant augmentation in the regularity of the societary action, in the freedom and happiness of our people, in the strength of the government, and in the confidence of the world, both at home and abroad, in the stability of our institutions. Such is the view that has been presented to you, in the hope and belief that to a lover of freedom like yourself it would be one of the highest interest, and that it would be met and considered in a manner worthy of a statesman and a Christian. Has it been so considered? To an examination of that question I shall now ask your attention, reserving for a future letter the consideration of the effects of the advalorem system in producing those financial crises whose terrible effects you have so well depicted, and that pauperism and crime whose growth you have so much deplored.

The experience of the outer world is in full accordance with our own, the whole proving that the tendency toward harmony, peace, and freedom, exists in the direct ratio of the diversity in the demand for human force, and consequent power of combination among the men of whom society is composed. Therefore is it, that the most distinguished economists are found uniting in the idea expressed by M. Chevalier, the free trader whom you so much admire, that it is only "the accomplishment of a positive duty" on the part of governments, so to direct their measures as to facilitate the taking possession of all the various branches of industry for which the country has been by nature suited. Such must be the view of every real statesman — recognizing, as such men must, the existence of a perfect harmony in the great and permanent interests of all the various portions of society, laborers and capitalists, producers and consumers, farmers and manufacturers. Of such harmony, however, you give your readers none—consumers of cloth and iron here being told that capitalists "not satisfied with their profits" are anxious to "increase the burdens of the people;" that "the fraternity of mill-owners," and they alone, are anxious for a change of system, with increase of taxes; that "the lords of the mills" are dictating to the Committee of Ways and Means; that "mill-owners have dictated the whole system of indirect taxation;" and that it is high time for them now to protest against the further maintenance or extension of the system. Here, as everywhere, you are found in alliance with that British free trade system which seeks the production of discord, and discord and slavery march always hand in hand together through the world.

Allow me now, my dear sir, to ask you if you really believe that the facts are such as they here are said to be? Do you not, as well as myself, *know*, that for years past, the wealthy mill owners of New England have been opposed to any change of system that could, by giving increased protection, tend to augment domestic competition for the sale of cloth, knowing, as they did, *that such competition must decrease the cost of cloth to the consumer.* So is it now, with the wealthy iron master. He can live, though all around him may be crushed by British competition; and then, in common with his wealthy British rivals, he must profit by the destruction they have made. Such being the facts, and that they are so I can positively assert, are you not, by opposing protective measures, aiding in the creation among ourselves of a little " oligarchy of mill owners," whose power to increase the "tribute money" of which you so much complain, results directly from the failure of Congress so to act as to increase domestic competition for the sale of cloth and iron? The less that competition, the less must be the reward of labor, and the larger the profits of the capitalist, but the greater must be the tendency towards pauperism and crime, and the less the power to consume either cloth or iron.

" Hitherto," as you here tell your readers, our people "have been oppressed by powerful and compact minorities." In this you are right —a small minority of voters in the Southern States having dictated the repeal of the protective tariffs of 1828 and 1842, and having now, with a single and brief exception, dictated for thirty years both the foreign and domestic policy of this country. In 1840, however, the free people of our Northern States, farmers, mechanics, laborers, and miners — the men who had labor to sell and knew that it commanded better prices in protective than in free trade times — rose in their might and hurled from power this little " oligarchy" of slave owners, then taking for themselves the protection which they felt they so greatly needed. That it is, which they now seek again to do — desiring once again to free themselves from the control of that " powerful and compact minority" of slaveholders, under whose iron rule they so long have suffered.

Permit me now, my dear sir, to ask on what side it was you stood, in the great contest of 1842? Was it with the poor farmer of the North who sought emancipation from the tax of transportation, by the creation of a domestic market for his products? Was it with the mechanic who sought the re-opening of the shop in which he so long had wrought? Was it with the laborer whose wife and children were perishing for want of food? Was it with the little shopkeeper who found his little capital disappearing under demands for the payment of usurious interest? *Was it not*, on the contrary, with that " little oligarchy" of men who owned the laborers they employed, and opposed the protective policy, because it looked to giving the laborer increased control over the products of his labor? *Was it not* with the rich capitalist who desired that labor might be cheap, and money dear? *Was it not* with those foreign capitalists who desired that raw materials might be low in price, and cloth and linen high? *Was it not* with those British statesmen who find in the enormous capitals of English iron masters "the most potent instruments of warfare against the competing industry of other countries"? To all these questions the answers must be in the affirmative, your

journal having then stood conspicuous among the advocates of pro-
slavery domination over the free laborers of the Northern States. —
We have now another free trade period, when crisis has been followed
by paralysis, and it may, my dear sir, be not improper to inquire on what
side it is that you now are placed. Is it by the side of the free laborer
who is perishing because of inability to sell his labor? Is it by that
of the poor farmer of the West, who finds himself compelled to pay five
per cent, *per month*, to the rich capitalist? Is it by that of the unemployed mechanic of the Middle and Northern States? Is it by that of
the farmer whose land diminishes in value because of the enormous tax
of transportation to which he is subjected? *Is it not*, on the contrary,
by the side of that "little oligarchy" which holds to the belief that the
laborer is "the mud-sill" of society, that slavery for the white man and
the black is the natural order of things, and that "free society has
proved a failure"? For an answer to these questions, allow me now to
point you to the fact that you have here invoked the aid of a Senate,
the control of which is entirely in the hands of that same "oligarchy,"
for resisting any and every change in our commercial policy asked for
by the farmers and laborers of the Northern States. Now, as for thirty
years past, your opponents are found among the men who sell their own
labor, while your chief allies are found in the ranks of those by whom
such men are classed as serfs. Need we wonder, then, that your journal
should be always advocating the cause of the millionaires, and thus
helping to augment the pauperism and crime whose rapid growth you
so much lament?

The facts being thus so entirely the reverse of what you have stated
them to be, is it not, my dear sir, most remarkable —

That, after aiding, during so long a period, in the establishment of
pro-slavery domination over our domestic and foreign commerce, you
should now venture to assert, that "the mill owners have dictated the
whole system of indirect taxation, ever since the late war with Great
Britain"?

That, the necessity for resorting to such mis-statements does not furnish
you with proof conclusive of the exceeding weakness of the cause in
support of which you are engaged?

That, regard for truth does not prompt you to a re-examination of the
question, with a view to satisfying yourself that of all the pro-slavery
advocates, the *Journal of Commerce* not excepted, there is not even a
single one that has proved more efficient than yourself?

Hoping that you may follow my example. by giving this letter a
place in your columns, and ready to place within the reach of millions
of protectionist readers, whatever answer you may see fit to make, I
remain,   Yours, very respectfully,
                                                HENRY C. CAREY.

W. C. BRYANT, ESQ.

                                        PHILADELPHIA, *February* 28, 1860.

LETTER TENTH.

DEAR SIR.—Allow me to beg that you now review with me some of the facts that thus far have been presented for your consideration, having done which, I will ask you to say if in the annals of the world there can anywhere be found a more admirable contrivance for the annihilation of domestic commerce than that which exists among ourselves, consequent upon the adoption of British free trade doctrines. Closing our mills and furnaces, the government compels our people to seek the West. There arrived, they find themselves taxed for transportation to such extent that not only have they no power to develop the mineral wealth that so much abounds, but are wholly unable even to construct roads by means of which to go to the distant market. Few in number and poor, they are driven to seek relief at the hands of their British friends, or masters, pledging their lands and houses as security for the payment of railroad bonds. In due season, the foreign creditor becomes owner of the road, anxious to increase his revenue, but, above all, anxious to promote the dispersion of our people, and to secure the maintenance of our existing colonial dependence. Seeking to accomplish that object, he taxes *your* farmers for the transportation of the produce of distant lands — compelling *them* to make good all the losses resulting from cheaply carrying the products of Wisconsin and Minnesota. Thus destroying the value of the land and labor of Atlantic States, he compels a further emigration, and thus on and on he goes — fully carrying out the British plan of recolonization, while always lauding the advantages to be derived from the British free trade system. It is a remarkably ingenious arrangement, and the more you study it, the more, my dear sir, you must be led to wonder at the folly of our people in having so long submitted to it. The British people are somewhat heavily taxed, but for every dollar they pay for the support of *their own* system, do not our people pay ten for the support of *foreign people and foreign governments?*

That the strength of a community grows as its internal commerce increases, and declines as that commerce decays, is proved by the history of every nation of the world. Such being the case, allow me to ask you now to look with me into that commerce among ourselves, with a view to determining its extent. How much does Kentucky exchange with Missouri? What is the annual value of the commerce of Ohio with Indiana, or of Virginia with Kentucky? Scarcely more, as I imagine, than that of a single day's labor of their respective populations; and, perhaps, not even half so much.—Why is this the case? Is it not a necessary consequence of the absence of that diversity of employments *within the States,* everywhere seen to be so indispensable to the maintenance of commerce? Assuredly it is. Ohio and Indiana have little more than one pursuit — that of tearing out the soil, and exporting it in the form of food. Virginia and Kentucky sell their soil

in the forms of tobacco and of corn. Carolina and Alabama have the
same pursuits; and so it is throughout by far the larger portion of the
Union — millions of people being employed in one part of it, in robbing
the earth of the constituents of cotton, while in others, other millions
are employed in plundering the great treasury of nature, of the constituents of wheat and rice, corn and tobacco, and thus destroying, for themselves and their successors, the power to maintain commerce.

The commerce of State with State is thus, as you see, my dear sir,
but very trivial; and the reason why it is so, is, that the commerce of
man with his fellow-man, within the States, as a general rule, is so ex-
ceedingly diminutive. Were the people of Illinois enabled to develop
their almost boundless deposits of coal and iron ore, and thus to call to
their aid the wonderful power of steam, the internal commerce of the
State would grow rapidly — making a market at home for the food produced, and enabling its producer to become a large consumer of cotton.
Cotton mills then growing up, bales of cotton wool would travel up the
Mississippi, to be given in exchange for the iron required for the roads
of Arkansas and Alabama, and for the machinery demanded for the construction of cotton and sugar mills, in Texas and Louisiana.

That, however, being precisely the sort of commerce which Britain
so much dreads, and that, too, which our own government desires to
destroy, the capitalist feels no confidence in any road dependent upon its
growth, whether for the payment of interest upon its bonds, or dividends
upon its stock. Hence the almost entire impossibility of obtaining the
means of making any road that does not lead directly to Liverpool and
Manchester. Look with me, I pray you, into the Report just now published, of the Sunbury and Erie Railroad — running, as it does, through
a country abounding in mineral wealth and fertile lands. Its length
is 288 miles, 248 of which are already made, and 148 completed by
the laying of the iron — the expenditure having somewhat exceeded
$8,500,000. There, however, the work stops, it being quite impossible
to obtain, even as a temporary loan, either at home or abroad, the trivial
sum that is yet required, except at the cost of sacrifices that must be
ruinous to those who have commenced the work. Until it shall be
obtained, the capital already expended must fail to be productive, and
lands equal in extent to a moderate German kingdom, must fail to contribute to the maintenance of our people, and to the increase of the
States in wealth, strength, and power.

Thirty years since, Germany did as we are doing, exporting raw materials, and importing finished products. Adopting protection, she has
placed herself in a position to compete with Britain for the purchase of
wool and cotton, and for the export of knives and cloth. Then she was
poor, but now she is so rich that her people take from us bonds by
which our roads and lands are bound for the payment of rates of inte-.
rest so enormous as to ruin the persons whose property has been pledged.
—Thirty years since, we paid off all our foreign debts. Adopting free
trade measures, we have since created a foreign debt that requires for
payment of its interest alone, more than the products of all our farms
that go to Europe. Then, we were rich and strong. Now, we appear
as beggars for loans in every money market of Europe, and are fast becoming the very paupers of the world.

That our system tends to the destruction of domestic commerce in the Atlantic States, is beyond a question. How it affects the value of land and labor throughout those Western States, in whose favor you now appeal to your Legislature, asking for a continuance of the system by means of which the New York farmer is made to pay the cost of transporting the corn and wheat of his Western competitor, we may now inquire.

Ten years since, Congress created in Illinois a great company of landlords — granting many millions of acres of land, coupled with the obligation to construct a road from north to south, across the State. Two years later, an ex-Secretary of the Treasury, author of the tariff of 1846, was found in London, engaged in peddling off the Company's stock and bonds. While there, he published a book, setting forth the fact that Illinois abounded in rich soils, and in coal and ores, and proving that the land alone would pay for making a road that was to cost, according to my recollection, some fifteen or twenty millions of dollars — the whole of which must, therefore, be clear profit to the stockholders. Eventually, the bait was swallowed, and the result exhibits itself in the fact that Mr. Cobden has been a ruined man — having been led by his free trade friends to invest therein the whole sum of $350,000 paid to him by the Manchester manufacturers, as compensation for his successful efforts at bringing about a repeal of the British corn laws, and of our protective tariff of 1842.

Why is this? Why is it, that the proprietors of so many millions of acres, and of a road crossing so many beds of coal and ores of various kinds, are ruined men? Because the road runs from north to south, and not from east to west, and cannot, therefore, be made a part of any line leading through New York to Liverpool. Because, the value of the land depended upon the development of domestic commerce — that commerce which "Britain has so much cause to dread." Had the tariff of 1842 continued in existence, the coal of Illinois would long since have been brought into connection with the lead, iron, and copper ores of Missouri, and the country of the lakes, and with the cotton of the South; and then, all the promises of Mr. Walker, and all the hopes of Mr. Cobden, would have been fully realized. Had, however, that tariff been maintained, the people of Illinois would have made their own roads, and the country would have been spared the disgrace of having ex-Cabinet ministers engaged in the effort to persuade English bankers to lend the money required for their construction. They would have been spared, too, a succession of financial crises, bringing ruin to themselves, while enabling their British free trade friends to denounce them, in common with all their countrymen, as little better than thieves and vagabonds.

The less our domestic commerce, the greater is our dependence upon Liverpool and Manchester, and the less our power to construct any road that does not lead in that direction — the general rule being, that north and south roads can never be made to pay. Look to your own State, crossed by two railroads, leading through your city to Liverpool, while your people are being heavily taxed for an enlargement of your canals, which has for its only object an increase of competition on the part of Western farmers; that increase, too, established at the very moment when your railroad owners are compelling your farmers to pay all the losses they incur in carrying Western produce at less than the mere cost of transportation. Passing south, you find a Pennsylvania road, running east and west, to compete with yours, Maryland and Virginia roads to compete with all, and South Carolina and Georgia roads intended to do the same; but of local roads you find almost none whatever. Why is this? Because Liverpool is becoming more and more the centre of our system, with New York for its place of distribution. Because we are fast relapsing into a state of colonization even more complete than that which existed before the Revolution.

For the moment, your city profits by this British free trade policy, the prices of lots rising as the taxation of farming lands augments, but, is it quite certain that her services will always be required, as distributer of the produce of British looms? May it not be, and that, too, at no distant period, that Manchester and Cincinnati will find it better to dispense with services that require the payment of such enormous sums as are now required for the maintenance of so many thousands of expensive families, the use of so many costly warehouses, and the payment of such enormous rates of interest? The Grand Trunk Road has already, as we are told by the *Daily Times,*

"Seized upon our Western carrying trade, and linked Chicago and Cincinnati to Portland and Boston *by the way of Canada,* and on terms which almost defy competition from the trunk lines of Maryland, Pennsylvania, and New York. They are delivering flour and grain in New England, and both domestic and foreign merchandize in Ohio and Illinois, cheaper than they can be profitably transported via Philadelphia, or New York, or Albany. Not content with this, they have entered into competition with our coasting-trade from the Gulf to the East, and, using that other Anglo-American enterprise just alluded to, the Illinois Central, are delivering cotton from Memphis to the New England factories cheaper and with more expedition than it can be forwarded by the Mississippi River to New Orleans, and thence by sea to New York and Boston. Nor have they been unmindful of their own direct steam communication with England from Quebec and Portland—the last-named point being converted into a mart of British-American commerce by reason of the perpetual lease or virtual ownership by the Grand Trunk Company of the Atlantic and St. Lawrence Railway from Portland to the Victoria Bridge. They are now using the Quebec line of screw steamers, already one of the most successful between England and this continent, for delivering produce from Cincinnati and Chicago at Liverpool *in twenty days!* — to which end they issue their own responsible bills of lading in the West *through to Liverpool.* A sample of this operation may be seen in Wall Street almost any day attached to sterling bills of exchange made against breadstuffs and meat and provisions from the West on England. And it is by no means certain that in another year the cotton of Tennessee and North Mississippi will not be made to take the same extraordinary direction, say from the planting States to Manchester through Canada."

Such being the case now, at the end of fourteen years of British free trade, what will it be ten or twenty years hence? Arrangements are already on foot for connecting Southern cities with Liverpool by means of Portland," while, throughout the West, the managers of the road "have not," as we are farther told,

"Failed to effect the needful alliances in the West, to make the connexions at least temporarily complete. The Illinois Central, from Cairo to Chicago, is their natural ally by reason of its English proprietary, and they bridge the peninsula of Michigan by another English work, the Detroit and Milwaukee Railway. As this last connection will not fully answer the designs of the company on the winter and early spring trade of the West, while the lakes are closed, it is not impossible that one of the older Michigan roads may be leased, like the Atlantic and St. Lawrence, or a controlling interest purchased in its shares and mortgages. The Michigan Southern has been named in this connection, because of its present financial embarrassments, which have cheapened almost to a nominal value its stock and bonds, and because, too, of its terminus at Toledo as well as Detroit; the former point being essential to the Cincinnati connections of the Grand Trunk."

The more frequent and severe our financial crises, the more perfect must become the control of British traders over all our roads, and the greater the tendency towards diminution in the necessity for profiting of the services of New York stores and New York merchants. So, at least, it seems to me.

For seven years past we have talked of the construction of a road to California, but, in the present state of our affairs, becoming poorer and more embarrassed from year to year, it is quite impossible that we should ever enter upon such a work. The wealth and power of Britain, on the contrary, become greater from day to day — all her colonies, ourselves included, being compelled to add to the value of her land and labor, while their own soils become more and more impoverished, and their own laborers are less and less employed. Let our existing commercial policy be maintained, and we shall see the Grand Trunk Road extended to the Pacific — Portland and Quebec becoming the agents of Liverpool and Manchester, and taking the place now occupied by New York.

Looking at all these facts, is it not clear—

That all our tendencies are now in the direction of colonial vassalage?

That, as your city has grown at the expense of others, because of its proximity to Liverpool, so other places, furnishing means of communication that are more direct, may profit thereby at its expense?

That as Liverpool has taken the place of New York in regard to ships, it may soon do so in regard to trade? And therefore,

That the real and permanent interests of your city are to be promoted by an union of all our people for the re-establishment of that industrial independence which grew so rapidly under the protective tariffs of 1828 and 1842?—

Begging you to be assured of my continued determination to give to the answers you may make to these questions, the widest circulation among protectionist readers, I remain, my dear sir,

Yours, very truly,
HENRY C. CAREY.

W. C. BRYANT, ESQ.

PHILADELPHIA, *March* 6, 1860.

LETTER ELEVENTH.

From the Evening Post, Tuesday, Feb. 28.

"An Example of the Effect of Protection.—Among the commodities which have hitherto not been permitted to be brought into France from foreign countries is cutlery. It is now included in the list of merchandize to which the late treaty with Great Britain opens the ports of France.

"Those who have made a comparison of French cutlery with the cutlery of the British islands must have been at first surprised at the difference in the quality. Nothing can exceed the perfection of workmanship in the articles turned out from the workshops of Sheffield. The symmetry and perfect adaptation of the form, the excellence of the material, the freedom from flaws, and the mirror-like polish which distinguish them,·have for years past been the admiration of the world. French cutlery, placed by its side, has a ruder, rougher appearance, an unfinished look, as if the proper tools were wanting to the artisan, or as if it was the product of a race among whom the useful arts had made less progress.

"This is not owing to any parsimony of nature, either in supplying the material to be wrought or the faculties of the artisan who brings it to a useful shape. The ores of the French mines yield metal of an excellent quality, and the French race is one of the most ingenious and dexterous in the world. In all manufactures requiring the nicest precision and the greatest delicacy of workmanship the French may be said to excel the rest of mankind. Out of the most unpromising and apparently intractable materials their skilful hands fabricate articles of use or ornament of the most pleasing and becoming forms. What, then, is the reason that their cutlery is so much inferior to that of Great Britain?

"In all probability the reason is that which at one time caused the silk trade to languish in Great Britain, which at one time made the people of the same country complain that their glass was both bad in quality and high in price. In both these instances the competition of foreign artisans was excluded; the British manufacturer having the monopoly of the market, there was nothing to stimulate his ingenuity; he produced articles of inferior quality, his vocation did not flourish, and both he and the community were dissatisfied. So with regard to the cutlery of France, the difficulty has been the prohibition of the foreign article. Let the foreign and the French commodity be looked at side by side for a few years in the shop-windows of Paris, if the duty to which cutlery is still to be subject will permit it, and we think we may venture to pledge ourselves that the French workmen will show themselves in due time no way behind their English rivals. We may expect the same result to take place which has so much astonished and puzzled the friends of protection in Sardinia, where the removal of prohibitions and protective duties has caused a hundred different branches of manufacturing industry to spring to sudden and prosperous activity."

Dear Sir:—Anxious that all the protectionists of the Union should, as far as possible, have it within their power to study both sides of this question, I here, as you see, lay before my readers your latest argument against protection, thereby affording them that opportunity of judging for themselves which you so systematically deny to the readers of the *Post*. Why is it that it is so denied? Is it that the British system can be maintained in no other manner than by such concealment of great facts as is here so clearly obvious? While enlarging upon the deficiencies of French cutlery, as resulting from protection, was it necessary to shut out from view the important fact, that under a protective system more complete, and more steadily maintained, than any other in the world, France has made such extraordinary progress in all textile manufactures, that she now exports of them to the extent of almost hundreds of millions of dollars annually — supplying them at home and abroad so cheaply, that she finds herself now ready to substitute protective duties for the prohibitions which have so long existed? Would it not be far more fair and honest were you to give your readers all the facts, instead of limiting yourself to the few that can be made to seem to furnish evidence of the truth of that system to which you are so much attached, and to which we are indebted for the financial crises whose ruinous effects you have so well described?

Why is it that the French people, while so successful with regard to silks and cottons, are so deficient in respect to the production and manufacture of the various metals? The cause of this is not, as you tell your readers, to be found in "the parsimony of nature," and yet, it is a well-known fact, that while the supply of coal and iron ore is very limited, others of the most useful metals are not to be found in France. This, however, is not all, the "parsimony of nature" which, notwithstanding your denial of it, so certainly exists, being here accompanied by restrictions on domestic commerce of the most injurious kind, an account of which, from a work of the highest character, will be found in the following paragraph:

"By the French law, *all minerals of every kind belong to the crown, and the only advantage the proprietor of the soil enjoys, is, to have the refusal of the mine at the rent fixed upon it by the crown surveyors.* There is great difficulty sometimes in even obtaining the leave of the crown to sink a shaft upon the property of the individual who is anxious to undertake the speculation, and to pay the rent usually demanded, a certain portion of the gross product. The Comte Alexander de B—— has been vainly seeking this permission for a lead-mine on his estate in Brittany for upwards of ten years."

Having read this, you cannot but be satisfied that it accounts most fully for French deficiencies in the mining and metallurgic arts. That such was the case, you knew at the time you wrote your article, or you did not know it. If you did, would it not have been far more fair and honest to have given all the facts? If you did not, is it not evident that you have need to study further, before undertaking to lecture upon questions of such high importance?

Turning now from French cutlery to British glass, I find you telling your readers that the deficiency in this latter had been "in all probability" due to the fact, that "the competition of foreign artisans" had been so entirely excluded. On the contrary, my dear sir, it was due to restrictions on internal commerce, glass having been, until within a few years past, subjected to an excise duty, yielding an annual revenue of more than $3,000,000. To secure the collection of that revenue, it had been found necessary to subject the manufacturer to such regulations in reference to his modes of operation as rendered improvement quite impossible. From the moment that domestic commerce became free, domestic competition grew, bringing with it the great changes that have since occurred. That such is the case, is known to all the world, and yet I find no mention of these important facts in this article intended for the readers of the *Post*. Would they not, my dear sir, be better instructed, were you to permit them to see and read both sides of this great question?

What has recently been done with British glass, is precisely what was sought to be done in France by Colbert and Turgot, both of whom saw in the removal of restrictions upon internal commerce the real road to an extended intercourse with other nations of the world. With us, the great obstacle standing in the way of domestic commerce, is found in those large British capitals which, as we are now officially informed, constitute "the great instruments of warfare against the competing capitals of other countries, and are the most essential instruments now remaining by which the manufacturing supremacy" of England "can be maintained;" and in protecting our people against that most destructive "warfare," we are but following in the direction indicated by the most eminent French economists, from Colbert to Chevalier. France has protected her people, and therefore is it, that agricultural products are high in price, while finished commodities are cheap, and that the country becomes more rich and independent from year to year. We refuse to grant protection, and therefore do we sink deeper in colonial vassalage from day to day.

Foreign competition in the domestic market is, however, as we here are told, indispensable to improvement in the modes of manufacture. This being really so, how is it, my dear sir, that France has so very much improved in the various branches, in which foreign competition has been so entirely *prohibited?* How is it, that Belgium and Germany have so far superseded England in regard to woollen cloths? How is it, that American newspapers have so much improved, while being cheapened? Have not these last an entire monopoly of the home market? Would it be possible to print a *Tribune*, or a *Post*, in England, for New York consumption? Perfectly protected, as you yourself are, is it not time that you should open your eyes to the fact that it is to the stimulation of domestic competition for the purchase of raw materials, and for the sale of finished commodities, we must look for any and every increase in the wealth, happiness, and freedom of our people?

The more perfect the possession of the domestic market, the greater is the power to supply the foreign one — the *Tribune* being enabled to supply its distant subscribers so very cheaply, for the reason that it and its fellows have to fear no competition for home advertisements from the London *Times*, or *Post*. "This principle," as you yourself have most truly said,

"Is common to every business. Every manufacturer practises it, by always allowing the purchaser of large quantities of his surplus manufacture an advantage over the domestic consumer, for the simple reason that the domestic consumer must support the manufacturer, and as the quantity of goods consumed at home is very much larger than that sent abroad, it is the habit of the manufacturer to send his surplus abroad, and sell at any price, so as to relieve the market of a surplus which might depress prices at home, and compel him to work at little or no profit."

Admitting now that it were possible for the London *Times* to supply, on every evening, a paper precisely similar to yours—forcing abroad the surplus, and selling "at any price, so as to relieve the domestic market," would you not be among the first to demand protection against the system? Would you not assure your readers of the entire impossibility of maintaining competition against a journal, all of whose expenses of composition and editorship were paid by the home market — leaving its proprietors to look abroad for little more than the mere cost of paper and of presswork? Would you not demonstrate to them the absolute necessity of protecting *themselves* against a "warfare" that must inevitably result in the creation of a "little oligarchy" of monopolists who, when domestic competition had been finally broken down, would compel them to pay ten cents for a journal neither larger nor better than they now obtain for two? Assuredly, you would.

Addressing such arguments to your British free trade friends, they would, however, refer you to the columns of the *Post*, begging you to study the assurance that had there been given, that—

"Whenever the course of financial fluctuation shall have broken the hold of monopolists and speculators upon the mines of iron and coal, which the Almighty made for the common use of man, and whenever there shall be men of skill and enterprise to spare to go into the business of iron-making for a living, and not on speculation, who shall set their wits at it to find out the best ways and the cheapest processes, it must be that such an abundance both of ore and fuel can be made to yield plenty of iron, in spite of the competition of European ironmasters who have to bring their products three thousand miles to find a market."

To all this you would, of course, reply, that "financial fluctuations" created monopolies, and never "broke their hold;" that men of "skill and enterprise" were not generally rich enough to compete with such rivals as the London *Times;* that domestic competition had already given us "cheaper ways and cheaper processes" than any other country of the world; that the freight of a sheet of paper was as nothing compared with the cost of editorship and composition; that all these latter costs were, in the case of the British journals, paid by the domestic market; that "the domestic consumers supported the British manufacturer;" that the quantity of journals consumed at home was so very great that their producers could afford to sell abroad "at any price"— thereby "relieving the market of a surplus which might depress prices at home, and compel them to work at little or no profit;" and that, for all these reasons, it was absolutely necessary to grant you such protection as would give you the same security in the domestic market as was then enjoyed by your foreign rivals?

Would not all this be equally true if said to-day of our producers of cloth and iron, coal and lead? Does the policy you advocate tend to place them in a position successfully to contend with those British manufacturers who "voluntarily incur immense losses, in bad times, in order to destroy foreign competition, and to gain and keep possession of foreign markets"? Can they resist the action of the owners of those "great accumulations of capital" which have been made at our cost, and are now being used to "enable a few of the most wealthy capitalists to overwhelm all foreign competition in times of great depression "— thereby largely adding to their already enormous fortunes, " before foreign capital can again accumulate to such extent as to be able to establish a competition in prices with any chances of success"?   Can it be to the interest of any country to leave its miners and manufacturers exposed to a " warfare" such as is here officially declared ?   Do not they stand as much in need of protection, for the sake of the consumers, as you would do in the case supposed ?   Does not your own experience prove that the more perfect the security of the manufacturer in the domestic market, the greater is the tendency to that increase of domestic competition which tends to increase the prices of raw materials, while lessening the cost of cloth and iron ?   Do not men, everywhere, become more free, as that competition grows, and as employments become more diversified ?   Is not, then, the question we are discussing, one of the freedom and happiness of your fellow-men ?   If so, is it worthy of you to offer to your readers such arguments as are contained in the article above reprinted ?

Holding myself, as always heretofore, ready to give to my readers your replies to the questions I have put, I remain, my dear sir,

Yours, very truly,
HENRY C. CAREY.

W. C. BRYANT, ESQ.

PHILADELPHIA, March 13th, 1860.

LETTER TWELFTH.

DEAR SIR : — Thirty years since, South Carolina, prompted by a determination to resist the execution of laws that were in full accordance with both the letter and the spirit of the Constitution, first moved a dissolution of the Union. Failing to find a second, she stood alone. Since then, all has greatly changed. Now, each successive day brings with it from the South not only threats but measures of disunion, each in its turn finding more persons in the centre and the North anxious for the maintenance of the Union, yet disposed towards acquiescence in the decision of their southern brethren, whatever that may prove to be. This is a great change to have been effected in so brief a period, and sad as it is great. To what may it be attributed, and how may the remedy be applied?

Before answering this latter question, let us inquire into the causes of the disease — for that purpose looking for a moment into the records of our past. The men who made the Revolution did so, because they were tired of a system the essence of which was found in Lord Chatham's declaration, that the colonists should not be permitted to make for themselves "even so much as a single hobnail." They were sensible of the exhaustive character of a policy that compelled them to make all their exchanges in a single market — thereby enriching their foreign masters, while ruining themselves. Against this system they needed protection, and therefore did they make the Revolution — seeking political independence as a means of obtaining industrial and commercial independence. To render that protection really effective, they formed a more perfect union, whose first Congress gave us, as its first law, an act for the protection of manufactures. Washington and his secretaries, Hamilton and Jefferson, approved this course of action, and in so doing were followed by all of Washington's successors, down to General Jackson. For half a century, from 1783 to 1833, such was the general tendency of our commercial policy, and therefore was it that, notwithstanding the plunder of our merchants under British Orders in Council and French Decrees, and notwithstanding interferences with commerce by embargo and non-intercourse laws, there occurred in that long period, in time of peace, no single financial revulsion, involving suspension by our banks, or stoppage of payment by the government. In all that period there was, consequently, a general tendency toward harmony between the North and the South, in reference to the vexed question of slavery — both Virginia and Maryland having, in 1832, shown themselves almost prepared for abolition. Had the then existing commercial policy been maintained, the years that since have passed would have been marked by daily growth of harmony, and of confidence in the utility and permanence of our Union.

Such, unhappily, was not to be the case. Even at that moment South Carolina was preparing to assume that entire control of our commercial policy, which, with the exception of a single Presidential term, she has since maintained—thereby forcing the Union back to that colonial system, emancipation from which had been the primary object of the men who made the Revolution. With that exception her reign has now endured for more than five and twenty years, a period marked by constantly-recurring financial convulsions, attended by suspensions of our banks, bankruptcies of individuals and of the government, and growing discord among the States.

What, you will probably ask, is the connection between financial revulsion and sectional discord? Go with me, my dear sir, for a moment, into the poor dwelling of one of our unemployed workmen, and I will show you. The day is cold, and so is his stove. His wife and children are poorly clothed. His bed has been pawned for money with which to obtain food for his starving family. He himself has for months been idle, the shop in which he had been used to work having been closed, and its owner ruined. Ask him why is this, and he will tell you to look to our auction-stores and our shops, gorged with the products of foreign labor, while our own laborers perish in the absence of employment that will give them food. Ask him what is the remedy for this, and, if he is old enough to remember the admirable effects of the tariff of 1842, he will tell you that there can be none, so long as southern commercial policy shall continue to carry poverty, destitution, and death, into the homes of those who must sell their labor if they would live. That man has, perhaps, already conceived some idea of the existence of an "irrepressible conflict" between free and slave labor. A year hence, he may be driven by poverty into abolitionism.

The picture here presented is no fancy sketch. It is drawn from life. This man is the type of hundreds of thousands, I might say millions, of persons of various conditions of life, who have been ruined in the repeated financial crises of the five-and-twenty years of British free trade and South Carolinian domination. Follow those men on their weary way to the West, embittered as they are by the knowledge that it is to southern policy it is due that they are compelled to separate themselves from homes and friends, and perhaps from wives and children. See them, on their arrival there, paying treble and quadruple prices for the land they need, to the greedy speculator who finds his richest harvest in free trade times. Mark them, next, contracting for the payment of four and even five per cent per month, for the little money they need, knowing, as they do, that we are exporting almost millions of gold per week, to pay to foreigners for services that they would gladly have performed. Watch them as they give for little more than a single yard of cotton cloth, a bushel of corn, that under a different policy would give them almost a dozen yards. Trace them onward, until you find their little properties passing into the hands of the sheriff, they themselves being forced to seek new homes in lands that are even yet more distant. Reflect, I pray you, upon these facts, and you will find in them, my dear sir, the reasons why the soil of Kansas has been stained by the blood of men who, under other legislation, would have been found acting together for the promotion of the general good.

Mr. Calhoun sowed the seeds of sectionalism, abolitionism, and disunion, on the day on which he planted his free trade tree. Well watered and carefully tended by yourself and others, all have thriven, and all are now yielding fruit — in exhaustion of the soil of the older States, and consequent thirst for the acquisition of distant territory; in Kansas murders and Harper's Ferry riots; in civil and foreign wars. It is the same fruit that has been produced in Ireland, India, and all other countries that are subjected to the British system. Desiring that the fruit may wither, you must lay the axe to the root of the tree. That done, the noxious plants that have flourished in its shade will quickly decay and disappear.

We are told, however, that the interests of the South are to be promoted by the maintenance of the system under which Ireland and India have been ruined, and which it is the fashion of the day to term free trade. Was that the opinion of Washington, Jefferson, Madison, or Jackson? Is it, even now, the opinion of those Southern men whose views in regard to the slavery question are most in accordance with your own? Are not Kentucky and Tennessee, Virginia and North Carolina, Alabama and Missouri, rich in fuel and iron ore, and all the other materials required for the production of a varied industry? Did not the domestic consumption of cotton increase thrice more rapidly than the population, under the tariff of 1842? Had it continued to increase as it then was doing, would it not now absorb a million and a half of bales — diminishing by many hundreds of thousands the quantity for which we need a foreign market? Under such circumstances would not our planters obtain more for two and a half million of bales than they now do for three and a half millions? Rely upon it, my dear sir, there is no discord in the real and permanent interests of the various sections of the Union. There, all is perfect harmony, and what we now most need is the recognition, by men like you, and by our southern brethren, of the existence of that great and important fact. In that direction, and that alone, may be found the remedy for our great disease.

Looking for it there, the effect will soon exhibit itself in this development of the vast natural resources of every section of the country — in the utilization of the great water-powers of both South and North — and in the increase of that internal commerce to which, alone, we can look for extrication from the difficulties in which we are now involved. Let our policy be such as to produce development of that commerce, and villages will become tied to villages, cities to cities, States to States, and zones to zones, by silken threads scarcely visible to the eye, yet strong enough to bid defiance to every effort that may be made to break them. British policy sought to prevent the creation of such threads — British politicians having seen that by crossing and recrossing each other, and tying together the Puritan of the north, the Quaker, the German, and the Irishman of the centre, and the Episcopalian of the south, they would give unity and strength to the great whole that would be thus produced. Such, too, is the tendency of our present policy, our whole energies having been, and being now, given to the creation of nearly parallel lines of communication — roads and canals passing from west to east through New York and Pennsylvania, Maryland, Virginia, and Carolina — always at war with each other, and never touching until they reach the commercial capital of the British islands. In that direction lie pauperism, sectionalism, weakness, and final ruin of our system.

Desiring that the Union may be maintained we must seek again the road so plainly indicated to us by Washington, Jefferson, Madison, Monroe, and Jackson, the greatest men the South has yet produced.

In common with Franklin and Adams, Hancock and Hamilton, those men clearly saw that it was to the industrial element we were to look for that cement by which our people and our States were to be held together. Forgetting all the lessons they had taught, we have now so long been following in the direction indicated by our British free trade *friends* — by those who now see, as was seen before the Revolution, in the dispersion of our people the means of maintaining colonial vassalage —that already are they congratulating themselves upon the approaching dissolution of the Union, and the entire re-establishment of British influence over this northern portion of the continent. For proof of this, permit me to refer you to the following extracts from the *Morning Post,* now the recognised organ of the Palmerstonian government :

"*If the Northern States should separate from the Southern on the question of slavery* — one which now so fiercely agitates the public mind in America — that portion of the Grand Trunk Railway which traverses Maine, might at any day be closed against England, unless, indeed, the people of that State, *with an eye to commercial profit, should offer to annex themselves to Canada.* On military, as well as commercial grounds, it is obviously necessary that British North America should possess on the Atlantic a port open at all times of the year—a port which, whilst the terminus of that railway communication which is destined to do so much for the development and consolidation of the wealth and prosperity of British North America, will make England equally in peace and war independent of the United States. We trust that the question of confederation will be speedily forced upon the attention of her Majesty's Ministers. The present time is the most propitious for its discussion. . . . . . If slavery is to be the Nemesis of Republican America—if separation is to take place—the confederated States of British North America, then a strong and compact nation, would virtually hold the balance of power on the continent, *and lead to the restoration of that influence which, more than eighty years ago, England was supposed to have lost.* This object, with the uncertain future of Republican institutions in the United States before us, is a subject worthy of the early and earnest consideration of the Parliament and people of the mother country."

Shall these anticipations be realised? That they must be so, unless our commercial policy shall be changed, is as certain as that the light of day will follow the darkness of the night. Look where we may, discord, decay, and slavery, march hand in hand with the British free trade system — harmony and freedom, wealth and strength, on the contrary, growing in all those countries by which that system is resisted. Such having been, and being now, the case, are you not, my dear sir, in your steady advocacy of Carolinian policy among ourselves, doing all that lies in your power toward undoing the work that was done by the men of '76?

Repeating once again my offer to place your answers to this and other questions within the reach of a million and a half of protectionist readers, I remain,   Yours, very respectfully,

HENRY C. CAREY.

W. C. BRYANT, ESQ.

PHILADELPHIA, *March* 21, 1860.

www.ingramcontent.com/pod-product-compliance
Lightning Source LLC
Chambersburg PA
CBHW022156020726
47496CB00008B/2749